Saraceno

Djelloul Marbrook

Recital Publishing
Woodstock, NY, USA
www.recitalpublishing.com

An imprint of the online podcast The Strange Recital
Fiction that questions the nature of reality
www.thestrangerecital.com

for Dominick J. Guccione
1888 – 1959

When the Mafia don Gran John dubs Billy Salviati, his half Irish, half Italian hit man, *Il Saraceno* (sah-ra-CHAY-no), it's a compliment. He means Billy is competent and dangerous, loyal and enigmatic. He also means Billy is an outsider, a man born outside looking in, a marked man, as well as (in Mafia parlance) a made man.

The word Saracen began to be widely used in early Medieval times. It referred both to the Middle Eastern Arabs and to the Arabo-Berber peoples of North Africa, who were also called Moors. Implicit in European usage of the word was the idea of menace. In fact the Saracens were threatening the Medieval Europeans. That usage can be heard today in the score of the 2005 Crusader film *Kingdom of Heaven*.

Whenever the music turns menacing it refers to the Saracens. But to the Sicilians, who enjoyed a long period of prosperity and peace under Saracen rule before the Norman conquest of Sicily, the word has other connotations. And this is the context that to this day the West has chosen to frame its view of the Arabs: dangerous, menacing, the Dark Other of Jungian thought. Not surprising. After all, it's the way the Old Testament describes the Arabs, Hagar's children: they roam the wilderness, their hand raised against everyone, and everyone's hand raised against them.

SARACENO

~1~

Luck has bad breath.

That's what the Schwartzbear said, before they carried him out feet first. Billy was still on his feet the day he got out. He'd done hard time and more solitary than most and had no luck. Why think about it now? But he did. He thought about luck and the panther he'd been dreaming about.

He stood squinting outside Dannemora. Billy's out, he told the panther patrolling his mind, Billy's out. Too late, he heard poor Schwartzbear say. Get it? Schwartzbear asked. Now he got it—the panther is blind.

He no more knew why he stood there menacing a blind figment than he knew about luck. It just felt okay on a day better than most.

Then he slipped between pale June blocs of Franklin County light and was gone.

Big deal. No sweat. He was out of something more impregnable than Dannemora: the bestiary of childhood, and now he walked clean out of that rabid zoo towards the southern lights, a twisted communicant of roaches.

Maybe it was his dolphin's humor that did it—ask the merchant seamen who play their boom boxes for them to tell you how dolphins look and smile, hold your eye, show their tricks.

Sure Billy thought of animals, he'd been one, tanked with insects, cetaceans, raptors, reptiles, bottom feeders and alien species. One of them, the estimable black man Franklin Jones, had parked a conundrum in his head. "Lookitum," he'd said, "an'mal crackers, know what I'm sayin'?"

"Ya gonna tell me, arncha?"

"People be like an'mals, only dey an'mal crackers."

"Crazy?"

"Yeah, but dey crazy like differn' an'mals."

He had on his mind something more vivid. A dream. A recurring dream. He kept changing. He was a panther, then he was watching the panther. He could smell this panther, share its hunger, its rage and frustration. And one other thing, he couldn't remember when he awoke that he saw anything when he was a panther.

"I'm tellin' ya, Franklin, this panther is blind."

"What differns it make, Billy Boy? When this panther smell you, he be eatin' you. You not gonna care he be blind. Panther, all he know you be food."

Billy read the library out of panthers. He charmed the librarian into luring panthera pardus from the county library.

It became his meditation. As the yogi banks his eyes up in his head in his quest for samadhi, Billy contemplated his dream, and finally he saw the panther pacing, twitching its tail, behind the barred eye of his mother Frankie and the barred eyes of all his other keepers, and at that moment he could no longer be counted among the nations of predators licking their chops in their childhood zoos. He'd figured out there's no difference to them between food and keeper, between food and you. The most perfect animal shits. Despite our beautiful faces and elegant minds, we shit and die.

Billy once had a dolphin's spirit, the spirit of amusement, before it was beaten and cowed, but by the time he was eleven he had the sardonic eye of an elephant, dour, fixed.

In Dannemora—Billy's file called him a violent psychotic— a psychiatrist gave him a metaphor for his predicament.

"Think of your childhood, in fact think of everything up to now as a burning, smoke-filled movie house. What do you do? Figure out where the exits are, right?"

Dannemora certainly convinced him only the observant survive. "One thing more," the shrink told him, "imagine yourself as if you were nine or ten. You have to get that kid out of the burning building, that's your job. Understand?"

"What's playing?" Billy asked.

What can I say to any of these guys that will make a difference? Herschel Schwartz thought. He was by the time he met Billy sick of the question and the questioner. Maybe he'd have stuck around if he'd known the next thing he would say would make a difference. But by the time it did Herschel Schwartz had blown the roof of his head off.

"It's your question."

"Dumbo," Billy said.

"It's your life, asshole, not mine! Think! See if you can think for the first time in your life."

"Frankenstein?"

"Come over here to the window. Yes, I think I may see the light of an intelligence in your eyes. You think you're wising off, but let me tell you something, Mister Wisenheimer, you just put your money where your mouth is, d'you realize that?"

This tired old Schwartzbear interested Billy. What the hell was he talking about?

"Horror shows. You got it, smart ass. Horror shows. So ask yourself who showed you these horror shows. Whuh, you just naturally like to see people tortured? Or maybe somebody taught you how to like to see people tortured? Including maybe yourself. Got it? No? Well, think about it. You got lotsa time."

The stinking panther lodged in Billy's brain long before Frankie began her autoerotic visits. What a crock she was he knew but suppressed until one day in the fifth year of his confinement as he walked back to his cell block he heard a mocking in his brain.

Are you awright, Mom? I'm gonna take care of you when I get out, don't worry.

That's what he said, but what he heard in the choir stalls of the damned was please love me, Mom. "Please!"

"Please what?" the guard said.

"Please shit!"

So the next time Frankie came and said she couldn't stay long because Larry-What's-His-Face was waiting outside, Billy looked. And he looked. And the words came to him. Panther shit. And he laughed and looked some more until it seemed to him it was the first time he had ever looked, and he saw that it wasn't his cage he was looking through, it was hers. He saw the panther, the stinking panther pacing behind the bars in her eye. He heard her talk—she didn't hear him talk. Ever. It was her soap opera. And while she looked over her shoulder into the tarmac distance where Tom, Dick or Larry stood, Billy picked the lock of his childhood bestiary, the door swung open and he was free.

Right there in Dannemora.

"Get outta my face!"

"Hey, izzat any way to talk to yer mudder?" the guard said.

"You wanner, you kin' have 'er," Billy said. "Cheap."

Too bad Billy didn't see the guard quash a conspiratorial grin.

~2~

If anybody cared they might have said what made Billy dangerous by the time he checked into Arnie Besele's flophouse on Ninth Avenue was that he could do four hundred pushups a day or that he had taught himself a lot about electricity, but what made Billy dangerous was that he knew the only thing a panther knows is maul and eat. All your words, all your deeds, your care and willingness to love is nothing but meat and slop. The panther prowls the space between telephone calls, letters, obsessions, broken promises. You're fast food. Walk out. Some mother built that cage long ago of her inability to love. Once her little panther is your obsession you're its crank. Your sane moments merely threaten it with cold turkey. This is what Billy knew. Thank you, Frankie, thank you, Tom, Dick, Larry.

All in all, Dannemora straightened him out. He owed the poor dead Schwartzbear, Franklin Jones and the other fascinating basilisks, griffins, trolls, centaurs, Minotaurs, harpies, satyrs and rocs in their skulks, swarms, poufs, coveys, nests, pods, gams, nyes and gaggles, a big debt.

What he didn't owe them were his powers of concentration.

Dolphins look, elephants look, panthers gauge, but on the first free morning of his adult life, after seven years buffeted in the roaring night surf, Billy looked up from his nest of cockroaches to the fuming sun thrashing down Forty-Third Street and became the morning's namesake beast, a tiger. As to the difference between tigers and panthers, ask

5

any game warden who has seen a tiger's immense solar face in his windshield.

God knows what some paid priest will prate over Billy's grave, but of all his deeds and misdeeds this signal accomplishment will go unsung. In the land of Mom, Old Glory and apple pie we don't hang people for kissing off rotten parents, but we don't hang medals on them either. Mostly, with any luck at all, we whomp up enough money for a shrink to tell us we're panther shit.

Drink plenty of water, take long walks, move to the other side of the country. Or the world. Otherwise, you, the one man in the world who can rescue her, will find yourself hand over hand in Rapunzel's tresses, and the next thing you know you're staring a ravening panther in the face. More seductive than all the sirens are the human beasties roving your childhood pleading with you to let them out: Rapunzels and panthers, sleeping beauties and frog princes, fairy godmothers and kingly brothers. All of you waiting for your fetid ships to come in, consider how many shrinks and shrunk have committed suicide trying to rescue you!

Herbie Goldberg was a trickster, a joker, a squat Clark Gable, altogether decent. A week after he hired Matt Pieto to the night shift at the three Goldberg brothers' cigar store at Forty-Fifth and Eighth Avenue he said to him, "So Matt, what're you, slummin'?"

"Nah, I'm comin' up in the world, Herbie." With a straight face, a sincere look even, he said it.

Disarmed, Herbie schlepped around in the deep sink saying, "Yeah, well, when ya get to the top remember me."

Disarming, Matt was disarming even then, nineteen years old, a junior at Saint John's. No, he didn't need the job. His grandfather thought it a distraction, like athletics, inimical to the purpose of college, which was to get smart. But Matt, who never took a test that didn't amuse him, saw Hell's Kitchen as advanced study. He loved it, not having to live there.

Billy had lived there all his life, knew the Goldbergs as an easy mark, knew all the other easy marks, and, when nine months after Matt started to work there and seven days out of Dannemora he showed up one night to ask for a job, he'd cased the scene, watched Matt from across the avenue and was drawn without knowing it to this quiet kid who seemed to listen to everybody's story. Why were they telling this kid their stories? The rum-dumb boxer who dashed out into the street to pop windshields, tetchy bag ladies, loonies and drunks of every stripe, even the sons of bitches in blue?

"So what kin' I do ya?"

"I need a job. I grew up around here."

"That's a recommendation?"

"I'll work hard. I need a break."

"Why do I think you been vacationin' upstate?"

"I'm an ex-con."

"Hey, I need an ex-con like I need another health inspector. You don' look like no soda jerk t'me."

"What's a soda jerk look like?"

A tall pale goombah with a pompadour and duck's ass, that's not what Matt saw when he looked up. He saw the blackest, most fixed gaze he'd ever seen. Fixed on him.

"He don' look like no wise guy."

Amused by his boss's innocent term of art, Matt looked down the marble counter past Herbie at Billy's adz-cut face, eerily handsome. Billy gave him a little crooked smile.

"I think you should hire him, Herbie."

"Y'know him?"

"I will."

"Yeah, well, just do what my father here tells ya," Herbie told Billy, liking Matt enough to take the chance.

They worked in relative silence for two months. Three hundred and sixty of the *Daily News*, three hundred and forty *Mirrors*, fifty of the *Times*, forty *Tribunes*, hundreds of eight-cent egg creams and big green five-dollar Cuban Cohiba cigars from the humidor, night after night. Herbie liked his boys, drew coins from their ears, told them raunchy jokes, learned he could leave early trusting them to lock up.

"Gentlemen Dagos," he would say, "goo' night, keep everythin' kosher, don' sell the place, have a cigar, goo' night, sweet prinzes." Then he would bow and exit to Fort Lee. Matt and Billy would reach for the Cubans and finish up in a haze of blue smoke.

~3~

Their friendship deepened one night after Herbie left when Billy, sounding like a statue some conjuror-priest had moved to speak, said, "So boss, y'ever get laid?"

"What's it to ya?"

"Diddly."

They smiled, but Billy would remember he'd failed to daunt this boy. His study of Matt Pieto took a turn.

Each night at ten-thirty Billy relieved Matt at the newsstand out front. Matt would take the hand truck and wheel up Eighth to The Garden where he had a following.

The routine called for picking up the *News* and *Mirror*—the Garden crowd was not *Times* or *Tribune* caliber—selling all he could and trucking the rest back to the stand for sale. You had to be fast and have a certain personality. New Yorkers don't buy papers from bad faces.

Whuddya read, whuddya read?
Costello one, feds zip. Cards bomb
Pat Ward lookin' good, talkin' good,
take a look, take a look, she got a l'il black book!
Oleo heir says high-priced lookers
just go on dates—cops say they're hookers
Getcha papers, getcha papers
Ho-hum, ho-hum—Yanks win again
Putt-putt-putt—Ike goes golfing again—
Democrat says, Thank God!
Whuddya read? Buy two, don' be cheap!

One night as Matt was chanting this 1920s spiel outside the Ziegfeld the dancer Gwen Verdon, her head full of the schmaltzy *Kismet*, heard him and stopped to listen. Matt looked up from his change-making and, startled by her zany, boisterous beauty, rattled his head like a gourd in appreciation. She laughed, skipped over to him, tousled his hair and kissed his cheek, one of those lovely gestures that graces a life to its end.

Back at the stand each night Vivian Blaine and Robert Alda, playing the interminable *Guys and Dolls*, schussed up in a stretch limo and gave Matt a fiver for the three-penny *News*. At first Matt turned in all the two-penny, ninety-seven-cent and other tips, but when Herbie discovered this impeccable accounting he said, "Matt, one thing you ain't is a Hebe."

"Some of my best friends are Hebes, Herbie," Matt replied.

"I'm gonna make ya a honorary Hebe—keep the change from now on." It was not entirely generous. Matt had almost doubled news sales.

All this Billy took in with more attentiveness than Matt gave his professors. It was not just his usual acuity, it was more like having heard an unfamiliar melody and listening for it again.

Saturday nights called for heavy lifting. The Sunday papers weighed four to seven pounds, so Billy accompanied Matt to the truck drops. On one of these nights Matt tried to draw Billy out: "So wudja do time for?"

"What're you, my mother?"

"You had one?"

Billy surprised Matt by smiling thoughtfully. What kind of college kid would smart-mouth a guy who'd done hard time? And when he left off considering that, he found he had respect for the question. The answer was no, but he was no more ready to tell Matt that than he was ready to say he'd almost killed a cop. What the hell, he thought, the kid's awright.

"You wanna be my mother, douche a lot."

"Fuck off, Salviati!"

That did it. This kid acted like he was packing. It did it for Matt too, that skanky vulgarism. Time had not yet granted Matt the dispensation to see through such arrant machismo.

This dogleg in the course of their relationship proved decisive. Matt chugged on amiably but Billy circled until one quiet Tuesday night Matt returned from the *News* drop in front of The Garden with his left cheek laid open, his eye socket red, blue and yellow.

"Whudju run inta da truck?" Billy asked.

Matt made an ice pack and kept on working in the manner of a good wife beaten for the first time.

That Saturday night, as they pushed their hand trucks up the sidewalk, Matt said in the precise way he talked about anything serious, "The deal is the *News* driver cuts the bales—they come wired in fifties—he takes fifteen or twenty off the top and sells them on his own. When I bitched he changed my face."

"What about the others, the *Mirror* and the *Times*?"

"No, just the *News* guy."

Billy took his toothpick out of his mouth and spit with practiced accuracy down a grate.

As they neared the big sinister truck, which reminded Matt of a panzer, Billy put the flat of his hand on Matt's chest, staying him. He walked over to the high cab and pounded on the door.

"I wanna talk to you, Beverly."

"B-e-v-e-r-l-y?" Matt lip-synched.

The jowly teamster looked down at Billy. "Lissen, Slick, do I look like I got time for tea with delivery boys?"

"Make time."

Beverly took a menacing breath and started to transfer his gut out of the cab. Billy slammed the door on his left shin. The teamster hit the pavement in a pained crouch. Billy drop-kicked his face like a veteran place-kicker. Spitting blood, the man braced his back against the truck just in time to catch a roll of nickels in his rubber gut. He flailed at Billy hoping to connect, but Billy grabbed his hair and rammed his head into a lamppost, finishing him with a side-winding right. Just as Matt drew a sigh of relief to see it finished, Billy stomped the driver's gut. "You owe us a lotta money, Beverly!" Billy was using the guy's hair to slam his head on the macadam. He rifled his victim's pockets, took out three wads of bills in rubber bands and without looking at them said, "This ain't enough, what're ya gonna do?"

"How much den?" the terrified man said.

"Two extra bales a night from now on. Yeah, and say yer sorry to the nice man there."

"I'm sorry," the driver told Matt.

"With f-e-e-l-i-n-g, Beverly!" Billy said, kicking the man's ribs.

"I'm sorry, honest."

"I believe it," Matt said.

He watched Billy as they stacked the hand trucks and when he caught his eye Billy shrugged.

"So now we sell 'em on our own?" Matt asked.

"Nah, the boss made ya a honorary Hebe, didn't he? So we share."

Billy had recaptured Matt's attention. But no bond formed until he'd witnessed two more samples of the Salviati style. The first involved the acned brown-toothed kids who snatched papers off the newsstand to hustle them in bars. If Matt chased them, their confederates scooped up more behind him. Since it only happened between eleven and twelve, the height of the ink rush, Billy had not experienced it. But as Matt boosted sales it became necessary many nights for Billy to join him behind the stand. A few days after the extortion at The Garden two kids swam through the crowd and swiped about twenty of the *News*. Never the *Times* or *Tribune*. You couldn't hustle them to drunks. Billy slipped his thumb and forefinger into his mouth and piped a screech that stopped three cabs. The thieves turned to see Billy hefting a ten-pound lead pie used to anchor papers in the wind. "Hey kid, ya t'ink ya kin' run faster'n dis?" The little turds meekly brought the papers back. Billy whacked the first kid upside the face a bit too hard for joshing. "Ya wanna grow up 'n be a asshole like y'ole man?"

Matt gave Billy a troubled look.

"How'd I know his ole man's a asshole? Whuddya t'ink, dese are troubled y-o-o-oths from Tarrytown? Dis whole place's a kindergarten for Dannemora."

Matt nodded sadly. Billy knew.

Then there was the Marlon Brando incident which in years to come Matt would choose to think helped shape the actor's concern for underdogs. Brando—this was before fame found him *On the Waterfront*—was a chintz who pissed Matt almost every night by holding his hand out poker-faced, waiting for his lousy two cents on a nickel while maybe two dozen other people were trying to put money in Matt's hand. It was a New York convention, a source of nightly satisfaction, to give the kid the two cents, or maybe seven or even twenty-two. But *The Wild One* apparently saw no reason to discriminate against Billy. Billy, when it happened, looked at Brando's hand, then he looked into Brando's face, then, lighting up as if he had misunderstood but now understood, he took Brando's hand in his, turned it back and forth like a palm-reader, and said, "Nice hand. So, whatsamatter, ya don' believe in givin' to the poor?"

The dark shade that descended over Brando's face halted about two thirds of the way down, then snapped back up with a chuckle. The next night he ignored Matt, waited until he could give his nickel to Billy and cheerfully walked off without his change. Characteristically, Billy turned to Matt with a wry grin, "Ya t'ink he could spare a dime?"

$\sim$4$\sim$

Matt caught a left hook sparring in the college ring when it came to him that Billy's handling of the truck driver had taken up a low orbit among his thoughts. Shaking off the punch, Matt suddenly knew what made Billy effective. Billy's mind didn't wander. Probably it had nowhere better to go. Matt grew up in a world of effective men, but none of them had Billy's concentration. He was a man with whom you did not end conversations saying, *Capiche?* What you had to gauge with Billy was how much he got you hadn't said.

They now worked together whimsically. Observing this, Herbie one night shouted through the sliding glass panels between the store and newsstand, "Hey you two paisanos, y'in love? We gotta maka da money! Y'know, gelt?"

Billy Salviati had damn-near killed for lesser remarks, but now he looked to Matt for response. Matt leveled one of his studious, bemused smiles at Herbie. "It's paisani, Herbie, paisani."

"Paisani/schmyzani, sounds like cheese t'me," Herbie said.

Banter was not Billy's style. He rightly knew it masked issues, but if it was okay with the kid he'd try it.

"I don' t'ink Herbie wants to be a honorary dago, Matt."

As if Billy had forgotten it, Matt said, "He's a good man."

Sometimes Billy would leaf respectfully through Matt's books.

"So dis guy Spinoza, he was a paisano?"

Occasionally he would stop in on his day off with some spectacularly glitzy showgirl from *Guys and Dolls*. He'd be wearing a navy blue camel's hair coat, a silver tie with jacquard shirt, and pointy patent shoes. He'd invite Matt to join them after work and, although Matt always pleaded homework, the two did fall into the habit of beer and pizza at Patsy Mariani's on Tenth Avenue. Patsy also owned a masonry company that did a lively business losing stiffs in walls and floors. In this latter capacity he knew Matt's grandfathers well and would talk Sicilian to Matt while Billy, catching few sentences, would listen appreciatively, wondering why his father Pete, who checked out in a knife fight in Attica when Billy was three, hadn't cared enough about him to stay alive instead of referring him to Irish Frankie.

Submarine contemplations rarely eluded Matt's sonar. He was a student of their signatures, as one growing up in his family ought to be. On one such occasion, while Patsy was shoving pizzas into the kiln on a long wooden paddle, Matt asked, "J'ever wonder what happened to my old man?"

Billy looked like an old trout studying a new lure.

"Loco. He almost killed me and my mother. My grandfathers sent him back to Sicily when I was eleven. One day he was gone. Vavoom! Never heard from him again. With his temper, he's probably dead."

Billy could hear his heart. He felt like DiMaggio watching for the right throw in 1941.

"Yer grandfather's an important man."

"This is news?"

Checked but not deterred, Billy said, "I'd like to meet him. I mean, ya know, like pay my respects."

Matt made three rings on the table with his beer glass. He let the importance of this to Billy sink in.

After a long silence, Billy asked, "Can do, Matt?"

Matt looked at him with mathematical dispassion. He felt as if he'd been asked to grow up too soon. He felt respect for the seriousness of Billy's petition, for the softness of it. And he felt dread. "Si."

Nine days later in front of John Altobene's house on the south side of Nineteenth Street between Second and Third Avenues Matt felt something like the spacey chill and fever of first love when he saw Billy, who'd gotten himself up like a college boy: gray herringbone jacket, red and black striped tie, a blue Oxford button-down, twills, no coat. He'd gotten his long black hair cut close. He'd copied Matt. Now he looked to him for approval. Matt, with his nuncio's politesse, figured it would be rude to acknowledge this transformation. Billy was his elder, had suffered, extended himself for Matt. Matt turned his palm up and motioned Billy up the sandstone steps.

"Matteo, Nonno."

"Come back here, bring you fren' wichu."

They passed through a dark Victorian parlor, sliding acid-etched glass doors to a dining room, then the kitchen: headquarters. Gran John was at the double sink. He had a Parodi in his mouth. He was wearing suspenders over an undershirt. He blew a thin, thoughtful line of blue smoke in Billy's direction, appraising him. He picked up a squid. "Calamari, you like calamari?"

Billy looked apprehensively at Matt.

"Matt, he likes calamari, I'm askin' you."

"Gran..." Matt said.

"Y'Italian, arncha? Matt, whudda we got, a non compos mentis here?"

Like a Zen archer Billy moved forward and knelt in front of the old man and kissed his fishy hand.

"Jesus," Matt breathed, but John looked at his grandson with a wry smile and crossed his lips with his forefinger. Centuries passed between them. This was not the fealty of love Matthew owed the old man, but it was fealty, and in it the half-breed Billy was more Sicilian than his young benefactor.

John put his wet hand under Billy's chin and elevated him. They were both tall, but Billy was taller. John's ghostly blue eyes, the Norman strain, ransacked Billy.

"Siddown. I'm gonna feed you the best meal you ever had. You don' look like you eat too good."

Matt was aware if Gran John was not that Billy hadn't uttered a word. "Gran..."

"What, you' needle stuck, Matteo? You usually a very quiet boy, but you gotta learn just 'cause somebody else don' speak is no reason you hafta fill up the space. *Capiche?*" He patted Matt's cheek. "This is my boy, Billy." He had never said it before, nor was it lost on Matt he said it now, nor on Maria, who watched this scene from the pantry. "Maria, this is Mr. Billy Salviati. Guillermo, this is my daughter Maria. Respect her."

They had noticed each other and knew it was no time to let their eyes linger.

"Sit down, Mr. Salviati." Maria poured wine.

Still not a word. Now Matt was in awe of Billy, of the ceremony taking place.

"Matthew," she said, "you look tired. I think you work too much. Does he work too much, Mr. Salviati? He comes home with his face cut up, is this a life for a college man?"

Billy looked to Matt for help.

"Maria, the boy wants to know things. They don' teach him everything in that college. He's awright, he knows what he's doing," John said.

Then the old man and his daughter, practiced like dancers, cooked and served together, their bodies fond, deferential.

When finally he sat John became voluble. He spoke of his youth on Elizabeth Street, of selling papers on cold nights in front of Luchow's on Fourteenth Street, which was then uptown, of the swells and their ladies, of the despicable Irish and their ill treatment of fellow Catholics, of Salvatore Maranzano and Charlie Luciano. "Lucana, forgive me, Lucana, that's his name." Maria and her son had heard it all, but in Billy the old man had a rapt audience. Matt noticed that Billy sipped his wine with restraint, like a communicant at Mass.

"Mr. Salviati, we speak both Italian and English here, so if you'd like to try a few words we won't bite your head off," Maria said teasingly.

"You never heard of *omerta*, Maria, nice Italian woman like you?"

"I'm speaking about a little dinner conversation, Pa, I want to hear about Mr. Salviati."

"Women," John said, "if you let 'em they gonna be the death of you."

"I don't think any woman is going to be the death of Mr. Salviati, Pa, he's too handsome."

John's turn for discomfort. Billy was not for Maria, God knew. Then he had an inspiration. "This man here suffered a lot. You know about suffering, Maria. You wanna hear his story, it gonna make you sorry you asked. You don' drink, Billy?"

Billy's lips tightened. He felt love for this old man who'd sized him up so well. It was his turn to show he knew something about John.

"When you drink you give the other guy the drop," he informed his calamari.

"Ha, so that's a chapter out of his book, Maria, you happy?"

Maria saw Vito and Charlie and Joey and a long line of others before her. She shuddered.

"I'm happy, Pa."

Matt wondered if that could be. She'd married a dangerous man to find he was not half so dangerous as her father or all those other men who sheltered and protected her. How would she ever find a man? How could a beautiful woman in her prime, who with her son provided her father with all his meaning in life, reach out and choose another life? Matt and

Billy exchanged a look of complicity that tricked Billy's mouth sideways in rue. The gesture entered Matt's life like an IV. He felt despondent as when the priest elevates the host and he remembers the crucifixion. This encounter seemed like the Last Supper, the despair. And hope. Whose last supper? Billy's? Was Matt Judas? He hoped not, as much for his own as Billy's sake. And yet where else was Billy prepared to go?

"So Matteo, tomorrow you take Billy here to see Carmine, tell him what I said."

"Whudju say, Gran?"

The old man reached over to Matt beside him, held his face in both hands and nodded.

~5~

Synchronicities, if we knew their number, would scare us. As it is, they cloy. For example, just about the moment a caustic August sun slumped like a tired scout in a Parthian saddle over the Palisades, Billy Salviati met Hettie Warshaw on West Forty-Sixth Street, while over on Nineteenth Street two old men talked about him. That itself was rare because in the nine years since Billy met John Altobene he'd become a man you had to meet, desperately didn't want to meet, or was the last man you did meet, and in no case a man to talk about.

"He's like a mirror," Gus Pieto was saying, "one side you see yaself, the other side you don' see nuthin'."

"Better you don' look in that mirror," John said. He loved these Billy puzzlements.

Matt's grandfathers, much as they loved hating each other, came to enjoy each other's company, which had ramifications in Vegas, Hollywood and Malta, to name a few places. They're like kids, Matt mused, the thought disquieting, as were all signals of his grandfathers' mortality.

"Ya know what I call him? Saint Lucifer," Gus said.

"So I heard," John said. His own sobriquet he kept to himself.

"Thank God he works for you."

"Yeah, you should thank him, Gus."

"Whudduz he do, does he eat, does he sleep, does he screw around? He's like a, a...."

John laughed, he owned the right word, but he never told anyone how he acquired it, not even Matt or Maria. It came

21

from Domenico Giovanni Altobene, his father, tinsmith, sculptor, puppeteer, a foolish, talented, loving man, incompetent to cope with life in America, which was, he told John, too detailed. And yet he'd been a man of details. For example, his puppets got him in trouble with the church. He made such an exquisite crêche their second Christmas in America that lines of people, some of them Russian Jews, wrapped around the block out onto Houston Street to peep through a hole in the door of the Altobene flat to see it. This competition for the attention of the immigrants exasperated the priests, but when they remonstrated with Domenico, he said, "You charge, I don't charge. Would Christ charge?" This irreverent response drew even more ire, but John remembered it fondly. And it was his father's puppets John recalled when he considered Billy, for Billy reminded him of the Saraceno with whom Sicilian mothers threatened their recalcitrant children. John's mother, Madalena, who died of tuberculosis that second year, had warned him, "Be a good boy or the Saraceno will get you."

"And what will he do with me?"

Chuckling at his son's curiosity, his father Domenico had said, "He'll make another Saraceno out of you, foolish boy."

"Ah Domenico!" his mother had cried.

But now John remembered those magical puppet shows—the pumped-up bravura of the Knights Templar, the death-ward competence of the infidel Saraceni—and he savored his secret.

Eventually Domenico returned to Sicily, wooed a well-born young nun out of her cloister, and lived happily ever after on the money young John sent.

John loved his father's story too much to part with it.

It was eight-thirty. Billy was walking west toward Ninth Avenue. He was thirty-eight years old, only a little heavier than when Matt met him. He was carrying a bag of groceries. He had taught himself how to cook. He was a good cook, but only Connie Larimer knew it. She was the bartender at Mina's in the Village. Other women he visited an hour, a day, a week, less and less, now hardly ever. Only with Connie had he shared meals in his spartan walkup in the Kitchen. Something of her prideful hunger moved him to feed her.

He could have moved, he could afford to, but he owned this rotting Kitchen where he was born. His mind as he walked, toothpick in mouth, set out the spectrum of vegetables he would need for tabouli, a dish Billy, always the abstemious eater, had grown to relish on summer evenings. Perhaps if he knew Gran John's secret sobriquet for him and knew tabouli too was Saraceno he would have relished it. Billy relished everything Gran John said. Because of Gran John he had a vocation, respect, money, and what someone he had yet to meet would call *weltschmerz*. All in all he was ahead of the game, but at that moment Hettie Warshaw was not. She was flat on her piquant po-po against a lamppost defending her brocade handbag against two muggers.

"Be nice boys, nice boys don' hurt a old lady," she pleaded. One of the muggers, a piggy albino who looked like he'd been dipped in fat, was twisting her left arm up her back toward her neck. The other, a ferret, was yanking the bag.

Billy considered the scene. "Yeah, be nice boys," he said as he set his bag down. Then, flowing like water, he drove his toe up into the ferret's balls. The ferret lurched around in an excruciated crouch, giving Billy the chance to grab him by the hair and smash his knee into his face. When he turned Piggy showed him a switchblade bloodied by the sun.

"C'mon, hotshot."

Billy smiled deprecatingly and showed him a nine-millimeter Beretta. Piggy paled. "Awright, awright," he said, chucking the knife.

In fast-forward takes that Hettie would try the rest of her life to erase Billy jammed the Beretta into the thug's mouth and hammered the top of his head with his free hand.

"Enough awready, Mr. Handsome Knight!" Hettie piped. "Are you the wrath of God?"

"Y'awright?" Billy asked, putting his hands under her arms and lifting her.

"I seen a lot woise den 'dis," she said, brushing her skirt down over what she called her petticoats. "Dis is a piece of cake, mister. I'm gonna call the pleece."

"Nah, forget it. Ya put 'em in jail ya gotta feed 'em." He turned and picked up his groceries, kicking the ferret's ribs.

Hettie grabbed his arm. "Wait a little minute here, Mr. Tough Guy." She was thinking what to say. Billy waited. "You look like you don' eat. You come wit' me, I'm gonna feed you like a cossack. An' don' gimme the look, experts gimme the look. Ya gotta date? I'm better than a date."

"I bet you are," Billy said.

Hettie fingered his shirt buttons as if looking for a mnemonic key. "Ya don' look Russian, you Russian? No, I don' t'ink you Russian."

"Why should I be Russian?"

"'Cause Russian is the last time anybody saved me."

"My name is Billy Salviati."

"Save this, save that, don' mean a t'ing, I know a good man when I see one. My name is Hettie Warshaw. Ya know what a Hettie Warshaw is? Is a yiddashalady, a millinery lady, is gonna feed you a nice meal, put some flesh on yer bones."

Billy shifted his toothpick. "You like tabouli?" he asked, nodding at his bag.

"Sure I like tabouli. You make tabouli, ya gotta have a glass of tea wit' it, maybe some nice baklava." She linked her arm with Billy's and tugged him. "C'mon, Mr. Billy Salviati, we gonna be friends."

~6~

Hettie was not what she seemed that thick August night. She was a magus. Her interrogative speech in the New York mode, redolent of Yiddish, was not the language of her adventurous mind, nor even her tongue once Billy got to know her. Billy had rescued a parent.

Hettie's apartment, only a block and a half from his, enthralled him: from its fluted baseboards to its articulated moldings it was chock-a-block with books, thousands of them, and maps, records, crystals, little replicas of propitiatory Egyptian statuary, Greek votaries, Sumerian scribes. No woman, no misery, no hope ever held him like this revelation that a human being, a humble human being, would want these things, need them, choose them, treasure them. He lived by figuring things out, by discovering what was coming down. What was coming down here? Where was the profit?

"Foist you fill the glass half with sugar, then you add some mint, then you pour from way up here," she said, climbing a one-step stool and pouring his tea from a silver carafe into a tall glass on a coffee table. "It's from the steppes, you know the steppes? You don' know the steppes? C'mon, I show you." She pulled a map of the Soviet Union from a hive of tubes crammed with rolled maps and showed him the grassland steppes. "Hot, hot, it's hot, you know hot? Hot is what Arabs on their camels say, giddyup, giddyup," she said, flicking imaginary reins.

Billy made tabouli. "It's not gonna be so good, it's s'posed to marinate," he told the bright blue eyes peering at him from their Tartar sockets in an alcove by the kitchen.

At dinner amid the books and maps the diminutive Hettie spoke of her girlhood in a Polish shtetl, of her parents' murder in the camps, of her marriage in Manhattan to a handsome chemist, a Mohawk who dived head-first one evening from their tenement on Jane Street when he learned Hettie had betrayed him with her boss.

"Why did I do that? The boss, Mr. Herman, his wife died, his children were nasty. He was so kind, so nice, so tired. Maybe I loved him too. So what's wrong with that, if I loved him a little? There isn't so much love to go around, you know."

Billy didn't notice that her street accent was receding.

"But Robert was young. Robert Hoskins was his name. He didn't understand. I didn't understand. Me, I didn't understand. I just knew Mr. Herman deserved a little love, and I had a little love to give him. He treated me like a daughter when I came here. I had nothing. Oh yeah, I had this tattoo and the clothes on my back is what I had. And memories, oi such memories! I was pretty."

Billy could see that.

"I worked so hard. I was good. I even designed hats for Mr. Herman. He loved them. They were funny. Fruity rich ladies bought them. So Robert died, then four years later Mr. Herman died, then I kept the shop, and when I had some money I retired, as they say. Yes, retired, myself, to read. I read."

Billy saw her as a child, a girl, a lover. Fair, supple, witchy, full of herself, headlong.

"You know what my biggest accomplishment is? Wut, wut, wut, that's what it is. Lissen t'me. Not vut. Oi it was so hard to learn double-u. Look at it even—it looks like two Vs! So when I stopped saying ven I said, Hettie, congratulations, you're an American."

"I have a secret, my handsome knight."

Billy fixed her with a smile that said, Hettie, we both know you have a lot of secrets.

"Yes, up there," she pointed to her ceiling. "Take your tea, you will see Hettie Warshaw's secret."

"How come you don't call yourself Hoskins?"

"Warshaw is a survivor, Hoskins is not, you think I'm a fool? A name is important. If you don't want to be it, you have a civil war on your hands. If it don't want to be you, you got *tsouris*. You know what *tsouris* is? Of course you do. I know. You got trouble."

"I got trouble?"

"You are trouble, Mr. Savior. But yes, you got it."

Jesus! Billy thought. He felt as if he were floating away from himself.

"Salviati," Billy said.

"Oh yes, Mr. Salviati, we have a lot in common. I don't wanna know what you do, but I know where you been. Yes, very strange, because you have a lavender aura, very spiritual. You kill people maybe. Big deal! I seen lotsa people killed for nuthin'," she said, readopting her manage-the-goyim accent. "Then I seen the killers killed. Big deal! You know what a aura is? I'm gonna show you your aura. Yes, I'll show you how to see auras if you want. It's a light around people. It changes. Very important."

She led him up the cement stairs to the sheet-metal roof hatch. When she lifted it he inhaled not the creosote fumes he knew and expected but a squall of perfumes. And floating in that black sea, illumined by the milky lights of the city diffused by night clouds, he saw row on row of roses, clustered polyantha, narrow-leafed, pungent, spear-leafed floribunda, tall hybrid tea roses, topiary roses, old roses, their profligate petals serrate, all bedded in vats of emerald Irish moss glistening with diamond-chip flowers. If he had seen roses before it was in galvanized pails on street corners. These roses were growing up out of that mysterium below.

How could anything be so perfect? It wasn't the word he wanted. He wanted a word that eluded him, wasn't even in his vocabulary: innocent. That was the scent in the air, washing his blood, the scent of innocence. He was excited when all that had ever come close to excitement in him was adrenalin. He joined the rosarian mania of the Romans who fretted that they hadn't left enough land for grain.

From that night there was in Billy a locus and in that locus the *prima materia* of the magus. The sorcerer chose her apprentice, the very soul of *omerta*, when neither had been seeking. He would come to understand these words and the Sufi saying, *when the student is ready the teacher appears*, no matter how strange their combined credentials. Any intelligent free woman would have given more than she could describe to win from a man what Hettie Warshaw readily won from Gran John's Saraceno. What his younger benefactor Matt Pieto longed for and missed in his elegant musings, Billy had walked straight into on Forty-Fifth Street in the shadow of his terrible birthplace.

"This is your aura—Angel Face," Hettie said, touching a lavender bud. "Yes, this is the color of your soul." She cocked her white head to his chest. "Your soul weeps. Yes, it's not your heart, it's a sob like a little baby's after he screams his head off and he can't cry no more. No, he can't make wet, just a little sob." She rubbed Billy's chest. "We have to take away this sob, it's a killer." Hettie looked up. She had to tilt her head back to see his face and in the corner of Billy's eye she saw an obsidian tear. She took a lace handkerchief from her sleeve—even in summer she wore long sleeves to hide the blue SS numbers on her arm—and tricked the tear from his eye.

Billy turned away.

~7~

To women Billy was a perfect if laconic gentleman, interested in what they cared to share, polite to their friends, and never wholly there or theirs. High-tone girls with androgynous names like Merrill and Leslie fixated on him. It was what he didn't say, didn't do, that itched their fantasies. To make inquiries of him was to assure themselves of the single clearest signal they would ever get. To make inquiries about him was next to useless. To tease him went a short way only. To try to anger him amused him. He never called, couldn't be called. Sooner or later all who cared not to live on the edge grew frightened, and those who hankered for the edge never saw it. Society girls could rarely resist surf-casting for him. Kitchen girls mooned, matrons ached. The sure way not to bait him was to insult some dude to impress him. There was no sure way.

As he aged he came to like flawed beauties, girls who didn't know they were pretty, aging women losing it, junior leaguers of icy demeanor whose hauteur smoldered under his gaze, brassy Joisey Goils whose makeup concealed their looks, Brooklyn doxies who walk like they're drying a manicure, and hungry-looking Kitchen girls pushing strollers and sporting shiners. And yet as he aged his body wisdom pulled the plug on his head. The head looked but the body malingered. Nor did he grieve. It had never been testosterone that drove him. Rather he followed the example of the incredible Sugar Ray Robinson, making up in cunning what he'd lost in speed. Boxing was the one sport he followed. He idolized

Sugar Ray, his equitable manner with men, his fuchsia Cadillac with its leopard upholstery and *femmes du jour* of every hue. He himself rented cars. He was not cunning in pursuit of women, he was cunning in surviving. Maria had been wrong. Billy broke no hearts, he haunted them. He had observed without being conscious of it that men who need conspicuous women are weak. They need to show off, to be surrounded by mirrors—invaluable knowledge to a man who studied men for a living.

By the time he encountered Hettie Warshaw Billy was ready to catch up with the ache no woman assuaged. He had paid Frankie off, certified himself a motherless child and been adopted by Sicilians.

"There's a whole lot of bread in this envelope," he told Frankie.

"You take it, you go anywhere you want, but you get outta New York."

"You own New York, big shot?"

With that he put the envelope back inside his jacket and stared at her. Frankie swallowed, reached into his pocket, withdrew the envelope, counted, and was gone.

That night Billy sat in Mina's and stared. He kept on staring until Connie came over with a fresh glass of seltzer and waved her hand in front of his eyes. He screwed up his mouth, drank, saluted her, put a twenty on the table, and left, kissing off, as Connie herself had done, a mean piece of karma.

Connie Larimer's was a third-stage beauty, the kind that ghosts some women in their late thirties, a wan, sad loveliness informed by pain and wisdom, a reward for prevailing, a poignant beauty not everyone sees. She had been the sort of tall blonde whose severity belies a natural humor. She seemed too remote to excite. Men thought her desirable without feeling desirous, a girl to be seen with. Now roughed up and reconstituted, this was her sexual moment and yet she felt only the need to be held dearly, to be loved, not to be made love to, not to be invaded. She wanted, when she arrived in Manhattan to study at Parsons, to design clothes, but her life was her single design, functional, workable. She could bear it. Victim of incest and abuse, she gravitated to seductive men who would help her reenact the family scene. In Joe Paquinette, the bass player she married, she found a man to beat, humiliate and rape her. One night, after booting and socking her around their apartment, tying her up and belting her, promising to come back after a few drinks with the band and give her what she deserved, she broke loose and ran into the street shoeless, shouting, "What do I deserve, what do I deserve?"

A police cruiser picked her up and took her to Manhattan South. There she met Sandy Morillo, a rape victim specialist.

"Getta grip," Sandy told her. She gave her a cup of coffee. "So whuddya do for a living, get your ass kicked? You think you need this schmuck to do it? Do it yourself, have a little dignity, kill yourself, for Crissake! You don't want to do that, do you? No, well, maybe you're not a dumb cunt after all. You wanna know what to do? Do you? Here, take this, take a hike, think it over, see these people, they can help you. I'm not big on talk. The more somebody talks the more a jerk like you thinks she can handle it. The next thing I know you're in the hospital, then it's the morgue. You wanna see the morgue? I can show you lots of women who thought they could handle it. He's really a nice guy, they say, only sometimes he gets mad. Mad? The guy's an asshole. Here's a mirror, look at yourself and tell me what a nice guy he is, tell me what you did to make him do this to you. Get outta here. Wait a minute. Lemme see your feet." She put a pair of old moccasins on Connie's feet. "Wise up. If you wanna talk some more, I'm here, here's my card. But don't come. Go where I told you. Okay?"

Connie nodded and left. She walked all night, down to the Battery, over to South Street, up First Avenue. At nine-thirty she used the change she had in her pocket to get a cup of coffee and drop a dime.

By ten two women from Lifenet on Hudson Street picked her up and took her to the shelter.

After eighteen months of therapy, talking to other battered women, learning how to bartend, she took a job at Mina's, and one night four years later she looked up from a steamy sink and saw Billy studying her. When their eyes met a tic snaked from the corner of her mouth to her eye. Connie had been one of those bewitched pubescents who stare shards in lieu of feelings. Perhaps the people—not always men—who drew this quirk pirated her back to some childhood trauma. Maybe it was racial memory. A black hooker once told her that she'd met this john, an A-rab she called him, a professor at NYU, he looked like a light sweet crude sheik, who made her face jump like that. Maybe he'd been a slaver in another life, she cracked. Response to her tic was usually as disquieting to the other person as it was to Connie, but Billy just smiled his crooked little smile.

"Lemme guess," trying to get back her composure, "rye neat?"

He said nothing. She shrugged and busied herself. "Seltzer and lime," he said. Other times he ordered espresso and a lemon twist.

"You recovering?"

"We're all recovering."

Billy was in the habit of buying for the sorriest drunks. He'd shuck them a stitchy brow, never speaking. When occasionally a rough crowd gathered, when some wazoo in gold chains jostled him, Billy moved over, said nothing. He'd just done this downrange of a boozy argument about baseball when one of the litigants invited him in. "So whuddya think, pal, they gonna wrap it up t'morrow or what?"

Billy shrugged.

"Hey, pardon me, mister, I axed you a question, you don' like sports?"

"I don' like sports, sport."

Connie, looking up from the sink over a harbor of bottles in a blue mirror, saw the big calzones heft their pork, heard the sound of machismo degaussing, felt Billy's eyes, shifted right to see him, and wondered for days if she'd seen him wink at her.

She had a little efficiency on Morton Street. She had a bike. Lifenet had gotten her a woman lawyer. She never saw Joe again. She cooked for the shelter days off. She read, tended bar, rode her bike, took in movies. She wasn't happy, but she was better than unhappy.

Bartending proved a good job for someone who had trouble with eye contact and yak. For a while she thought it was because dispensing something that made men so shamelessly maudlin gave her a sense of control, but then she decided it took her out of herself, gave her compassion, room to move around.

~8~

Connie's epiphany began in her support group at Lifenet two months after Billy's appearance at Mina's. Trying to recollect it, she knew Billy was on her mind that day but could no further connect him to what happened. She had invited Sandy Morillo to come that Saturday afternoon. The nine women knew each other, were important to each other but did not have the feminist literature that would come a decade later to frame their work. It was a muggy day early in September. The fan had given up and conversation degenerated into girl patter. Connie listened so hard it gave her a headache. Doris Flaherty was talking about some bozo who made the hairs at the base of her spine tingle when Connie erupted.

"This is meadow muffins."

"This is whaaa?" Doris said.

"Bullshit."

"Well, pardon me for living."

"Are you going to follow your nooky around all your life? Why don't you just pull your pants down and tell him, Here, grab a handful and I'll follow you anywhere?"

"Jesus Christ, Connie," Patty Contrera said.

"I want to lead with my noodle instead of my nooky," Connie said. "Does a man have special rights because he has a seven-inch dong that he can get up without my help? What can he do for me I can't do for myself? That's what I want to know."

"You need me to tell you, girl?" Patty said.

34

"No thank you, I'll figure it out for myself."

"And when you do you may be too old to appreciate it," Betty Washington said.

"Yeah, well, let me ask you somethin', gal," Connie said, drifting back to the high lonesome twang of her Appalachian home, "what's a bang worth to you? Is it that much better'n a good poop? Is it as blessed as peein' when you drink too much beer? Can any of you honestly say a man ever played with your titties better'n you can?"

"I can't suck 'em," Betty said.

Giggles.

"That's 'cause you ain't limber, girl," Calliope Simms said. "Me, I can suck mine sure as hell better'n some damned drunk."

Sandy and Connie caught each other's eye.

"Yeah, and I'll tell you what, what you think I be taking yoga for, you silly bitches?" Callie said, warming up. "Someday I'm gonna get my tongue down 'round my first chakra and I'm gonna kiss the man goodbye."

The women whooped uncomfortably.

"You be doin' it upside down, girl," Betty said.

"Upside down be better'n gettin' my beautiful black ass kicked."

"If there ain't no man out there thinks lovin' me's more important than dippin' his dong they kin' all keep their dongs and I'll keep my sanity," Connie said.

"So you can get the hots just looking at yourself in the mirror, Connie? What are we, a bunch of lesbians?"

"Damn right! I like what I see in the mirror. Do you? Lesbians I don't know, don't care, it ain't what I'm talkin' about."

"So let me ask you this," Patty persevered, "what does loving you mean?"

They savored the breadth of the question, Connie most of all. She may not have been leading with her noodle, but her mouth was equal to the occasion. "It means loving me even if I didn't have a twat or couldn't feel a goddamned thing when it's wham-bam-thank-you-ma'am. Me, not pieces of me. I don't need a dong to be me. I ain't seven inches deep, I'm a lot deeper and a lot smarter, and anything else is cattywampus."

Sandy the cop jumped up from the edge of their semi-circle and hugged and kissed her protégé.

Betty straightened her shoulders in indignation, she thrust her breasts and delivered herself, "We be talkin' lesbin' talk, this ain't no support group no more. I need a man to do me, girl."

"Did you hear yourself say that?" Sandy said. "Did you hear what you said?"

"I heerd."

"No you didn't, you said do me. That's what Connie's talking about. You here, girl, 'cause some man done you, did you forget that?"

"Don' nigger-talk me, Miz Pleecelady, 'cause you ain't one of the priv'leged few."

"Don't bullshit me, either, I want you to acknowledge what you said because your little black ass depends on it."

Betty stomped over to the window, turning her back on them. There was no eye contact in the room. After a long time she said, "I knowledge it."

Connie and Sandy walked over to her. They stood, the three of them, looking out the window while the others shuffled out.

Within the week Billy gave Connie a clue to the similarities of the sexes. Inopportunely trying out a macho schtick, she blew it off. He was sitting in the corner reading a Visconti Tarot deck. Connie thought he was playing solitaire. Wiping her hands on her apron she sat down opposite him and reached across the initialed, burned table for the hanged man. Quick as a cobra Billy grabbed her hand and took back the card. Unnerved, she said, "You a spook, Billy?"

"Don't do that."

"Don't do what?"

"You're not a ditz, don't act like one."

She went back to washing glasses. Then she came back. "I don't know how to talk to you."

"What's to say?"

"So I just look? And you look? That's it?"

"I got nothing for a lady like you."

"What's a lady like me?"

"It's your question, hang onto it."

More glasses. More customers. Then she took another pass. "I'm not a lady, I'm a broad been run hard and put up wet. Life's not a TV show, you know. I don't hang around here just to have bad dialogue with you."

"You don't have anything with me, lady," he said, and left.

Nice going, Connie, you blew it. You'll never see him again. And she didn't. For six months. Then one night about eleven-thirty he walked in, sat at the bar in front of her and picked up the conversation. "You wanna have something with me?"

Don't do it, Connie, don't say, What, after six months you think you can just come in here and... She didn't. "Yeah."

"How 'bout dinner Sunday night?"

"How come you know I'm off Sunday night?"

"I don't mess around."

"Does anybody ever mess with you, Billy?"

He took the toothpick out of his mouth, got up to leave, and said, "You're okay, Connie."

She didn't know why she felt so good, was it because Billy asked her out or because she'd grown up enough to just say yes?

It took Connie a long time to accept that a man who could lose himself in his music the way Joe did could lose himself in meanness. It happened this way: he always took his glasses off when the vibes started lining up—maybe it was that gesture that moved her to fall in love with him— then she remembered that he took his glasses off when he beat her. So the last time he beat her up she had to imagine Moe T. Brundage, the singer in whose group Joe mostly played, slamming the lid of his piano on her enthrallment. Yeah, she thought, Ole Moe (who'd been christened Molester), he'd a throwed hisself up if he knew his friend went home and whumped that high-tone lady of his. Moe didn't suppose class had anything to do with status. "I knowed cottonmouths got more class'n you," he once told a Fifty-Second Street club owner. Damn, how could a great soul like Moe love a sadist? Same way a steel-boned cougar-smart Appalachee gal could, she figured. Still, when you come down out of those torn-up hills passably beautiful yourself it's hard to accept what's beautiful ain't necessarily right. A man who could do jazz, which is everything to do with right, ought to be able to do right by a trusting heart. Yeah, forget that, Connie: any Nashville hack could tell you that, which is maybe why all that country caterwauling she hated as a girl began to win back her favor as a hard-run woman. Hell, if she'd wanted her ass kicked around she could have stayed home and hung out at the VFW and never followed the lights, the city's or her own.

"Appalachee gals fry a man's eyeballs till they marry," Moe'd told her.

"How's a Delta black man know 'bout Appalachee gals?"

"Black man do a lotta lookin' long's he jes' funnin'."

"And was you jes funnin', Moe?"

"Hell no, gal, I done live up to my foolish name."

They didn't say much at the table between sets when she took Billy to hear Moe but she could tell they liked each other. Billy liked a lot of people, a quality more sensual to her than being a good dancer or having senators kiss your ass. But it was his respectful way of liking people that whispered in her utmost hairs.

"Haven't you got any ego problems?" she asked him once. Christ, she'd thought, suppose he doesn't understand that stuff? So what am I doing with a guy who doesn't? Then she noticed that what's-your-game smile. She gave him her best c'mon-I'm-serious look.

"Can't afford them. Happy?"

"Scared shitless."

"Smart lady."

She could have pursued this dialogue all night long, but she knew it was distasteful to him. "Sorry, Billy."

His response was to make her aware of her buttons. They rose and she blushed and he smiled. Sadly, she thought.

~9~

In the five years Connie would witness the friendship of Billy and Hettie—she was their only real witness—she felt not envy but pride and remorse. Privilege too. She knew the little she shared with him—a dinner, a walk, a movie now and then—were not at Hettie's sufferance but her beneficence. In Hettie too she had a friend, however removed. Theirs was not a triangle but a circle, a Druid circle. Each of them had a place that could not be traversed in a spell broken only by Hettie's death in her sleep, maybe then not broken.

Connie had never known such peace, peace in the flow of wanting, and what she wanted was very little more than what she had—to be touched, her sole daring. Hettie Warshaw, Billy Salviati. Connie Larimer? And who was Matt Pieto, that courtly man so like and unlike Billy? For all her compulsive teasing him she knew better than to ask.

At an age when some women obsess about their biological clocks she was enthralled in place, listening to West Virginia and Sicily and Hell's Kitchen murmuring. And Dr. Josef Mengele.

Looking down at Billy touching the letters of Hettie's name on her stone plaque at Ferncliffe Connie remembered an afternoon when Hettie spoke to her of women, kitsch, Josef Mengele, a man born tired of women and syzygy. She had gone to see Hettie in the forlorn hope of glimpsing how much Billy there would be in her future.

Hettie had sized her up like a madam. And when she began to speak, Connie felt the need to fasten herself in.

40

"Some girls such a face they got on them it gonna make you kick your kazotsky with your head because you look twice," Hettie began. "Three times you look, your goose is cooked. I know such girls from way back. They take everything they own, they put it in a little safe in their head, they throw away the key and forget where the safe is. Hoity-toity girls they ain't. Hoity-toity girls got something to give. What these girls got is grief. You crack their little safes, that's what you got, grief. Now how you think Mr. Billy-Nothing-From-Nowhere-Salviati knows that? You gotta be somebody to know that. When I seen Billy knew that, I said, Hettie, this is a very old mensch.

"We play this game. I say, You like that one, Billy? and he says, She's awright. How 'bout that little tamale, and so on. Then I lay eyes on this black Irish girl, the kind that goes to Manhattanville College, her teeth are ruhvoised, the bottom ones look up at the top ones, but oi is she beautiful, she should be wearing boots and whipping kulaks. Billy? I says, and what does he say? He says, Forget that. That's what he says, forget that. So what does he mean? I think. He's not good enough for her maybe? And then I realize he means this cooky is bad luck. I realize this boy has lived a long time 'cause you don't see through such cookies with young eyes, my girl. Lotsa men gonna break their heads, not as to mention their other things, on a girl like that one. But Billy he was not born for women, he was tired of them already when he was born. You listening, Connie? This is a very tired man we got here. You want something from him you gotta be patient, you gotta be polite, and you still ain't gonna get what you think. What do you think, Connie? But maybe, may-be, you get something better. You wanna see stars you leave this man alone, you wanna friend maybe I'm gonna leave you one. But first you gotta line up your head and your heart and your little orphan pubey just like you are God lining up his planets for the whole megillah, which is called a syzygy, and that ain't so easy, in case you didn't notice.

"You never been here before, look around, see what I got. Don't be scared. Wait a minute! You should be scared. Why not? It's good for you. You know what fear is, is a straight arrow, points at what you have to do, where you have to go.

"Get me a little cognac over there. I don' like whiskey but I feel a little cold, I always feel a little cold when I'm gonna talk about the Joimans. They made Goethe, they made Bach, they made hell."

So what do you see when you look around? Is awright, you need a little help. See that man sitting over there? He's writing. Very important stuff, instructions for the dead, yes, like me. Please don't disturb him. I need his advice. See the man with the broken nose, that's Lorenzo Mister Magnificent, you look at him you feel strong. See Mr. Baudelaire over there, reminds you we're all crazy. You know who looked like him? Mister General Sherman. He was crazy too. A real Joiman, he liked order so much he killed everybody. Everything woiks. Yes, when I'm dead you walk around here—Billy I tell to let you—and you'll see, everything woiks, everything gotta woik, do its job. *Arbeit macht frei*—the Joimans weren't wrong about everything, y'know.

"You know why the Joimans did what they did, killed everybody? You think they went *farukh*? No. They weren't crazy. They did what the dead do. You think me, I'm *farukh*? Ah, that's good that cognac. The Joimans give you pneumonia. Everybody thinks the Joimans make everything woik, they gotta reputation. No, my Connila, their houses were full of schlock, kitsch, cuckoo clocks, nutty porcelain menageries that scare children, junk. They beat their kids and locked them in closets and collected junk. Why you think the Nazis closed the Bauhaus, you know the Bauhaus? No? Too bad, it was people who said you shouldn't live in a junkyard, everything should woik. The Joimans lived in a junkyard, in their houses, in their heads. They are a junkyard people. They beat their children's innocent little heinies to make them act like cuckoo clocks. This big rep they had, oh what a rep, for cleanliness—yes, yes, they cleaned their kitsch. The roaches even appreciated Ostpolitik.

"I seen them, Connila, those eyes. Dead. Yes, dead. This dead has a name. Revenant. You know what a revenant is? Is a Nazi. Dead but doesn't want to die, doesn't know how. You die after you live, you don't live, you don't die. This talk about Valhalla, the master race, we are all becoming the master race, they were becoming revenants. I used to think they were cowards, I was so glad to see those beautiful Russian boys kill them, but cowards is not a good word: a revenant can't be nothin'.

"I knew this man if that's what you could call him, a Dr. Josef Mengele. You heard of him maybe. I woiked for him. Before the war in Krakow I was a hospital administrator, so he used me. I was a kike but I was a pretty kike. I was fair, fair they liked, fair they thought was good, as in goodness, can you imagine that? Mengele they called the angel of death. He was a regular Dracula, charming, so considerate, oi the world is full of draculas.

"This guy Karl Marx, the one they're all so worried about in Washington, he says religion is the opiate of the people. I wanna tell you something, schlock is the opiate of the people. All religion does is protect people from spirituality. But schlock kills, my girl, it's a state of mind. Collectors are dangerous people. Lookit me, look around me, I'm a dangerous poisson. Oi did those Joimans collect! Every little cuckoo bird in every little Hansel und Gretel house worked. A Nazi officer, he looked like a Christmas tree. They did not understand that some things do not want to work. When they do not want to work, leave them alone. If God did not put it into your fragrant little lap, it is not for you. This I have to learn perhaps as the result of meshugeh God putting Dr. Mengele in my lap. Such a sense of humor she has, can anyone in his right mind imagine God with a schlong?

"I noticed something when I woiked for Mengele. I noticed a lot because everything was going to be the last thing I noticed. And I was very intent to hear God laugh. I noticed you look into a person's eyes you see this little doll. It's you, your own little round face. You can't pull a long face in some-one else's eye, did you know that? It's nice, it's a little funny, but most people don't look straight enough they should see it. So I look into Herr Doktor's face and I don't see nothing. So I look in all those revenants' eyes and I see the same thing, nothing. No little dolls. You disappear in their eyes. That is why you should look closely at the way people see you, be-cause most of them don't. Mengele sees me doing this, so he says, You're trying to hypnotize me, Hettie? For this he coulda killed me, drowned me in a tank of ice or peel off my skin. So I say, No, Herr Doktor, I am looking at my face in your eye. This he likes. Yes, it's called the pupilla, Hettie, he says. And I say to myself, So how come you don't have one, you golem?"

Connie remembered she had dropped like a coin into the sea of Hettie's words. She understood little but appreciated all. The old woman had suffered more than most of us, and she was more full of life until the moment she died than Connie or Billy could ever be. And she had cared about them, her revenants. She had cheated the angel of death to come care for the undead of America.

~10~

"You gave my regards to Oiving Boscovy?" A long strip of toilet paper was draped over Gran John's left shoulder, chevroned with whiskers and shaving cream. He brandished his favorite pearl-handled Solingen razor as he spoke.

"Yeah Boss, I gave him the Rolex."

"A watch is my regards?"

"I said, How is Missus Boscovy and little Phyllis and Sandy?"

"Thank you, Frank. And did Oiving have something to say to me?"

"Yeah, he gave me the books." Frank Turco held up an overstuffed red leather briefcase.

"Matteo, take the books to that suit you hired on Park Row, tell him I want a report, in one sentence, in twenty-four hours. Not twenty-five."

"Subito, Nonno."

"Did Oiving have something else to say?"

"Boss, he, he..." Frank jiggled from his belt up.

"Siddown, Frank. Matteo, give Frank a drink, let him enjoy."

Frank tried to fish up his story but every time it was about to break water he broke up and let go.

"I think it's going to be a nice day, Matteo. We are surrounded by friends, we give them a little shot, we make them laugh, and maybe pretty soon we even find out what the joke is."

"Sorry Boss, don't get sore, it's...."

"I'm not sore, Frank, I'm glad you having a good time, a man should enjoy his work."

Matt cast Gran a dark look.

"Sometimes," Gran amended.

"Boss, you know what a marine head is? Ooh Geez, I'm sorry, Boss..." He started burbling.

Matt looked disgusted.

"Matt, you got things to do maybe?"

He should have left, he usually did, but Gran John looked needy, so he shook his head.

"It's a terlet, Boss, a boat terlet. You take a dump, you push a little button, it chews it up and pow! it ends up in the drink."

"You ever hear of such a wonderful thing, Matteo?"

He didn't answer.

"This dumb cracker, if he sits on this little pot he could lose it up his ass he's so fat. He's got this humongous boat with poles stickin' out like the United Nations, you know, up First Avenue." He looked to John to be commended for this poeticism.

"See, we're makin' a diplomat outta Mr. Turco, Matteo. Ambassador Frank Turco, or maybe we'll make him a papal nuncio, you know what that is, Frank?"

Frank feared the old man when he was in one of these moods. Matt knew Gran was just trying to hold off the ineffable sadness of the thing.

"Take yer time, Mr. Ambassador, don't drink too fast." Each time he spoke he pulled his face for the razor. It sounded like hedge trimming to Matt, so much he hated the occasion.

Gran looked at Matt doubtfully.

"So this cracker, he woon't let anybody on da boat. Da Sheriff, he calls it Da Sheriff."

"What imagination."

"Anyway, so, according to Oiving, he takes a dump, he pushes da button and vavoom!"—Frank starts vibrating again—"it blows his ass off, right tru da top o' the boat—no boat, no sheriff, nuttin'."

"Nothing, Frank?"

"Da boat goes down like cement. Finito. He blew his own ass off, oh Jees...."

"A mercy killing," Gran John mused.

"You don' like it, Boss?"

"It's all right, Frank, a little simple, but it has a certain..." He looked to Matt, who thought of *je ne sais quoi* but said "poetry."

"Yeah, good, Matteo, poetry."

Matt felt soiled by this charade yet committed to play it out.

"Poetry, yes, life should have poetry, tell us about poetry, Matteo. What goes up comes down, what goes around comes around, right?"

"To every thing there is a season, and a time to every purpose under the heaven." Here Matthew skipped a verse. "A time to kill, and a time to heal: a time to break down, and a time to build up."

Matt's selectivity did not escape the old man. "Thank you, Matteo," he said carefully, "we can close the book now"—he reflected—"on this murdering bastard."

Matt thought back to the beginning of the story.

"Whack a cop?" Billy had said.

"Woozy Lomento, you know?"

"Yeah, happy little guy."

"He's not happy any more, I don't think."

Billy sucked a tooth. When Matt found the locus of Billy's stare he expected it to ignite. But he persevered. "This three-hundred-pound cracker sheriff down in Fontana, you know Fontana?"

"Havin' trouble with this one, Matt?"

"Yeah. Anyway, this turd—couldn't put his sunglasses on with a cigar in his mouth—he picked up Woozy for carryin'—for carryin' for Chrissake!—kicked his eyes out, little sucker bled to death in his cell. My grandfather wants you should"—it had to be said in the venerable argot— "he wants you should talk to him."

"Talk to him."

"Yeah. Talk to him."

"Been to any museums lately, Matt?"

"No, I haven't got laid for a while either. Talk to him, Billy. You got a problem?"

"You got a problem."

"What's my problem?"

"What're ya doin' this for, Matt?"

"What?"

"This. You're a...."

"Suit?"

"A gentleman."

"Do it, Billy."

"Whack a cop?"

"Here is his name, and some other stuff."

"If it was Carmine...."

"...we wouldn't be havin' this conversation."

"But Woozy?" Billy jerked his palms open.

"Gran John has his reasons." Matt thought of Gran John's fondness for Woozy but kept silent.

"An'?"

"I dunno."

Twice Connie set out to refill Matt's espresso, Billy's Pellegrino, and Billy had flagged her off with his forefinger. When he finally relented she said to Matt, "Mina's is honored by your presence." The two men leaned back and looked up at her in mock seriousness.

"So I should just try to look pretty, huh?" she said and shrugged.

"Geez, Connie," Matt said, "I didn't think you had to try."

His utter sincerity wiped her archness away. She walked off shaking her head. She would have bumped and ground naked on the bar to know what bound the men. She was a canny observer of men, how they sized each other up, bowed their legs and sailor-swaggered to the men's room, timed their moves, took things in, pumped themselves up: heavy lifters, toting their goddamned mannerisms around in a sweat. But these two: Billy the Cat, he took in everything and everyone unblinkingly. Matt the Aristocrat, you had to have a good eye to see him at all he was so unobtrusive. And one other thing, in a culture of gesticulators their hands were always still. One day she'd broken into a furious blush when she recognized that watching them was like discovering when she was a girl that she could get wet in anticipation. She could even imagine herself saying so to Matt—but not Billy—and him saying, What a lovely thought, Connie. He would say something like that, she knew. Better than a movie, she told herself, and maybe what she liked most was how pleasant it was to see two men rapt and uncompeting. It felt reassuring, a promise that not all men threatened or obsessed. Accordingly, as always, she warmed to the simple task of conveying how much she liked them, and, as always, they returned simple acknowledgment.

"Nothing has to happen, Connie," she told herself aloud at the espresso maker.

"One more thing," Matt said, "nothing happens until it happens." He'd come up behind her with his cup and saucer. She looked frantic.

"I talk to myself all the time, specially when I'm losing it," he said. "Sorry I embarrassed you, I admire you."

"I..." dammit, she needed to return a compliment he didn't need.

Seeing he'd flustered her, he went on, "We all see a lot more than we admit. I don't know what kind of world it'd be if we admitted all we see about each other, guess we're not ready for it."

I'm not a flibbertigibbet, I understand what you're saying, I'm ready for a world like that, she wanted to say. Then mercifully she managed to say, "Thank you, Matt."

"You're welcome," he said with a look that almost assured her he knew what she'd wanted to say.

When Matt left, she stared at Billy, always pale, looking drained. However much he liked, loved Matt Pieto, this night had ravaged him. Connie shook with longing. I just wanna be held, Billy, she crooned inside herself, I just wanna hold you, I don't care about anything else. She hugged herself, feeling everything else like a draft on her shoulders.

Some hairball down by the window was heading an old derelict out the door for the third time when Billy stood up and motioned to the poor wreck to come back and sit at his table. Connie came by. "Whuddya got in the kitchen for my nephew here?" The nephew looked disappointed, so Billy said, "He'll have a big whiskey, make it Jack Daniels, and then see what ya kin' find, okay?" The bum looked crazed with joy. After he took a belt, Billy motioned to the hamburger Connie had brought out, "Ya don' eat, ya get too sick ta drink." He held up the man's glass for another shot. This loosened the man's tongue, but Billy crossed his mouth with his finger and the old man fell silent. A less grateful man might have followed Billy's stare, but the two of them sat in amiable silence until Billy got up, put a twenty under his companion's glass, another under his own glass, and started out. When Connie called, "*Arrivederci,*" Billy merely nodded to himself and was gone.

~11~

Gran John broke Matt's meditation.

"Thank you, Mr. Ambassador, I appreciate your report. Take Missus Turco to Atlantic City, have a little vacation, don't drink too much, be a family man, I like family men, take my Lincoln."

"No kidding, Boss?"

"Yeah, you like ta drive it, doncha? Me, I like the subway. What's that story you told me, Matteo. You know, the Saraceno general conquers Persia and the king tells him sit, sit nex' ta me on this big peacock throne, and the general sits his ass down in the dust and he says, From dust I came and to dust I return, so while I live I shun't sit so high I forget. I like that story. Very much. You like it, Frank?"

"Yeah, Boss, it's a good story."

Frank gone, Maria, lost in her thoughts of Billy while the men had talked, combed her father's hair with her fingers, and began setting down a late lunch. "Veal piccata, Matthew, flat as paper."

He could not move his mouth.

"Your mother has a soft voice, Matteo, like snow falling."

"I'm sorry, Mama." She smoothed his brow with her thumbs.

For a guy who spent his life thinking, how the hell'd he miss so much? Did he really know what Maria was thinking, feeling, or did he only fear he knew? Did he care? Did Gran

51

John? Who the hell was there to care about anything? The answer bushwhacked him: he cared.

A triangle appalls itself, a square disdains its center, some sly Jesuit said so. Into his love for John, Maria and Gus he had interposed Billy Salviati, and now everything familiar spun out from the center of his life to the azimuth, and Matthew waited.

"I don't think you like my tomatoes that much, Matthew," Gran said. He'd been watching Toto, Gran John's dog, watering the plum tomatoes that bellied over tubs of white cascade petunias. He turned a torqued face to the old man.

"Oh, I see. A zip for a little loser, whuddid Oiving say, a schlemiel, 'zat whutchu think, Matteo? Nonno's losing his marbles? No, Matteo, I was young like you a long time ago, only I was stupid too. Jesus, was I stupid! I was like a truck—vavoom, vavoom, vavoom—I coulda ripped Gus apart like a chicken, yeah, Gus, you gran'father. But I didn't hafta 'cause I was smarter'n Gus. Sosa, you gran'mother, was a good woman, very good, she drove me crazy. Every day she went to mass, lisen'n to those lazy castrati. You know what that is? Course you do, you went to college. Me, I read *The Arabian Nights*, I love *The Arabian Nights* and Omar Khayyam. I followed his advice, take the cash and let the credit go, nor heed the rumble of a distant drum. You, you can heed the rumble of a distant drum. Is okay for you, you can afford to, I coon't.

"About Woozy, we din't call him Woozy then, we called him Dopey. Dopey Lomento. When he got smart enough to get confused we called him Woozy. Hey, he was glad we called him anything. He usta sit'n watch me alla time, you know, waitin' for somethin' to do. He ran errands. You coon't give him anythin' important to do 'cause he forgot. The most important thing he did was make his Adam's apple jump up and down and roll his eyes around in his head like one of those whatcha call 'em, pinwheels out in Coney Island. Make us all laugh when we had a problem, which was mainly you gran'father Gus. We hadda—like a joke, you gotta problem, refer it to Woozy, he's gonna solve it. Gus sells a little policy to one of our clients, Hey, Woozy, whudda we do? Then we all laugh and we go tell Gus, Gus, wit' all due respect, Woozy, our consiglieri, sez this gotta stop. Gus, who has not got a great sense of humor, he sez, Tell Woozy... and when the boys start to smile, you gran'father Gus he sez, Ah crap, youse guys don' know when to stop messin' around, and the boys say, That's the message.

"*Aspetti*, I was in love with this uptown girl. Yeah, Matteo, me, I was in love. Sosa I respected, love—that was somethin' else. Sosa was older'n me, big Spanish girl, like a plum, the first girl I ever slept with, so help me God, I was so busy I didn't have time to sleep. She got pregnant, so I married her. But this girl, she lived on Sixty-Third Street, near you in fact. Yeah, the real old money din't live on Park, just the empty suits. So this girl, she was one a' those with names like men. You know what her name was? Streater, Streater Simondson. Now what kinda name izzat for a girl? She shoulda loved Gus 'cause she thought if you was Italian you cracked heads; if you was Sicilian I dunno what she thought. She was low class, she had this big education, money, cars—LaSalle, y'ever heard of a LaSalle?—trips to Europe, but she was low class, only in those days she was like all those swells I usta sell papers to in front of Luchow's, she was... America, everythin' I wanted, beautiful, tall, cold, greedy. Yeah, greedy. She had everythin' and it was dirt to her. Everythin' was for kicks. What kicks, whuddid I know from kicks? You ain't Irish? I said to her. No, I'm sorry, I'm not, Giovanni, she sez. Giovanni, c'mon! That's good, I sez. What's good about it, she sez. I hate Irish, I sez. I'm gonna tell you a word make you laugh, Matteo. That's so quaint, Giovanni, she sez. So when I look up this word, because that's what I always do, it just makes me want her. Now that's quaint, right? What it shoulda done is make me wanna kick her ass—hey, I coulda missed, she hadda thin ass—but I was young, and I'm tellin' ya, this goddam country scared the crap outta me. I mean, who the hell could figure out what these swells wanted?"

"I think you figured it out pretty well, Gran."

"Yeah, but that was then. So, to make a long story short, this Streater Simondson hurt me. Bad. She cut me up like a piece of scungilli and spit me out. You know, we should live together, I sez. You and me? she sez. Darling, don't spoil everything, she sez. We have a lotta laughs together, that's all. So I get mad. I sez, whatsamatter, I'm not good enough for you? Somethin' like that, she sez, and that's it, she don't take my calls no more. I keep callin' her, me, no pride, nuthin'. You cold?"

This picture of Gran John was chilling.

"So I was sittin' down in the old club, you know, the Sons of Misilmeri on Mott Street, jes' sittin' like a stupido. I coon't eat, I coon't drink, I coon't sleep, I was like dead. The guys are sittin' so long they're beginnin' to look like finocchios and I din't know what to tell 'em. I din't care. And Woozy is sittin' there too, watchin' me like Toto. So I say, Get me some stogies, Dopey, and he gets up and he comes over t'me and he smooths my hair back like my mother usta, like Maria does. Then I don' see him for days. No stogies, no nuthin', he's so scared for what he done. I never forgot what he done. I mean, can you imagine a little loser like that doin' somethin' like that to his boss? No, Matteo, I never forgot. Whudda thing to do! Sosa hates me, the guys are scared shitless, me I feel like a eggplant, and Dopey Lomento pats me on the head. You get the picture, Matteo?"

Matt felt like a jet pilot nosing down over the horizon, pulling G's, weightless, gut in his throat. His grandfather's lust for a mean tart transformed itself in front of him to love for a hapless fool. It was—he wrestled with the recognition—Christian. His chest roiled, his eyes blurred with love of this old man, this attentive benefactor. But it was more than love, it was shame at having known him so little, having kept him trapped in a stereotype, just as Streater Simondson had done. Matt knew Streater Simondsons, and it was because of all Gran John had given him he was immune to them, and if he had an iota of Woozy's simple compassion he would find a way to tell the old man just that. Out of all that old hurt and pain John had carried with him, as if carrying a child from a burning house, an abiding love of a fool who had not been as foolish as he himself had been.

"Relax, Matteo, relax, I don' need you to say anythin'."

"I guess I'm growing up."

"Yeah? Well, take it easy, you got plenty a time."

"That's it, Gran."

Now it came.

"I got time because you made time for me. I know plenty of Streater Simondsons, but I never had to want anything from them. Because of you, I never had to sell papers to the swells or figure out what they wanted. You made me a swell."

John bent over the sink and chucked cold water up into his face. But Matthew had seen his tears.

"You look at somethin' for a long time, Matteo, and after a while, if you got smarts, you see that nuthin' is what it seems to be, nuthin'. And when nuthin' is happening some-thin's happening. *Capiche?*"

"*Io capito, Nonno. Io capito.*"

Gran John pinched his cheek. "You a good boy, Matteo, I woon'ta traded you for a hundred uptown bitches."

Or Woozy Lomento either, Matt thought.

He felt his mother's gaze.

When he turned her oval face was blasted like a flamenco singer's, her long green eyes unseeing. Billy, her face said, and once more the ground opened before him. From the start he'd chosen to file Maria's responses to Billy with those of dozens of other women. But at this moment everything one can call woman, not just aspects of a moment's choosing, fo-cused on Billy, seeing more than Matt saw. Billy had closed the circle opened by an uptown twit named Streater. Billy knew all about Streaters. None of them would have gutted him as that one had John. Matt nodded to his mother, it felt like a promise.

Class, John had spoken of class. Had he any sense of Maria's innate class? None of this was right, nor could he make it right. He could carry messages, but he could not shape them. He was a boy lost in a Fellini movie, he saw everything, could do nothing, or next to nothing, yet Maria believed he could.

He thought of Tasha Vernooy beading his Saville Row pinstripes with green mascara tears as she told him she'd lost Billy. She'd tried to brush them off, smudging his lapel.

"Let me buy you another one, Matthew," she'd said. "Oh please, I'd like to. But then you don't need anything, do you, Matthew?"

That was what he'd thought of her that night Billy first brought her to Mina's for a nightcap—she didn't need anything. Before Billy and Connie became friends. He'd drunk too much.

"Oh where have you been, Billy Boy, where have you been, Charming Billy?" Connie crooned.

Matt tried to eyeball her off that tack. But it was too late. "So ask me what I think of your girlfriend, Charmin' Billy," she said. "Have you been to seek a wife? Is she the darling of your life?"

Billy's cool always surprised Matt. "I think yer gonna tell me, arncha?" he said.

"Her eyes don't cry, her teeth squeak, and her bun's a pomander," Connie said.

Pomander sounded pretty good to Billy even if he didn't know what it was.

"J'you smell her too?" he asked.

Connie winked at Matt.

"Oh yeah. Joy at least. Fifty bucks a pop."

"Joy good, Matt? Matt here knows 'bout such things."

"Can't tell, Billy, never can tell. Gotta put it on, let it set, then you sniff. Everybody's skin's different."

Connie looked at Matt like she'd bitten off a rattler's head.

He thought of telling Gran John, who always liked a Billy story, about Streater Simondson's latter-day stand-in. Problem was, as much as he wanted to dislike Tasha, she'd wept on his lapel.

"Damn! How'd they do that?" Billy said when he first saw Tasha bearing her silver mons to The Goddess's stoup in the Cacique Villa.

So whimsical was his appraisal of her stately progress that she stopped, annoyed and amused.

"Do?" she arched a brow.

"I can't hear what you're saying when you do that?"

She examined the alien.

"You know, with your eyebrow," he offered.

Tasha laughed in spite of herself. "How'd they do that, you said, and I said, Do?"

"Yeah, you know, make something like you."

"Probably the way doggies do it. You know, with their tongues hanging out."

His turn to smile.

"You want to just keep looking, I'll give you a picture."

"I thought you had to pee."

"Did I tell you that?"

"You look kinda pinched."

Seeing they could go on like this, Billy Salviati of Hell's Kitchen and Dannemora and Tasha Vernooy of Rhinecliff and Fifth Avenue laughed hard and genuinely. That's how they started their thing, she compelled to be offended and sexualized by it, he admiring the porcelain. Humor glued them more than good looks.

Tasha never, as Connie had, contemplated Billy's long, artful fingers. He remained to her an Italian with quixotic connections. All Italians have quixotic connections to thin-nosed Hudson Valley heiresses with roots in high places. Had she considered those fingers' repose she might have followed her fear to the heart of something, but Tasha was content like her Dutch forebears in a thousand paintings to skate over the surface of everything and everyone. Accordingly, she would never savor that her bones, if not her humor, had once captivated the deadliest of men.

It ended as abruptly as it began, and only then Tasha Vernooy got serious, and only then was it Matt Pieto and not Billy who knew it. And now, having heard of Streater Simondson, sitting there savoring how much more beautiful his mother Maria was in every way, his mind played a trick. He felt sorry for Tasha Vernooy, sorrier for her than for Billy or Maria or Connie or John or himself.

And in that instant he remembered the rarefied moment when Billy noticed Connie Larimer. Really noticed her, from her good legs up, legs that looked perfectly turned in flats, noticed her tits were brave and her profile honest, her fey brown hair imperfect and welcoming. He'd watched Billy notice and thought of the end of the Tasha Vernooy thing.

They were in her Fifth Avenue apartment, Billy and Tasha. He'd never been there. He didn't want to be there. He didn't want her in Hell's Kitchen either. Or in Matt's apartment.

So there he was, oafish and pissed by the fireplace, holding a martini, not even wondering why she'd forgotten he hardly drank, waiting for her to reappear from somewhere. Instead she called. And called, a reedy-seedy call.

He stood in a hallway daze of doors. "What am I, a poodle?" But he followed her call and came upon a tableau saluting Rita Hayworth kneeling for *Life* on a silken bed in a black negligee. Rita was there, right there when she did it, and that's why thousands of GIs loved her. Tasha was somewhere else, watching her uninhabited double.

"*Amore,* I want to perform unspeakable acts on you. I want you to do everything to me."

His left knee locked as he shifted onto it. His hands hung at the hem of his jacket. Neither his toothpick nor his blood moved. She was heart-punch beautiful, but all that happened was words washing up like medical debris on the beaches of his brain: Dumb cunt... I'll give you unspeakable acts!

He looked out the window across Central Park to The Majestic where Frank Costello lived among the garment makers he extorted. Then he left, leaving as a memento mori the saddest face Tasha Vernooy would ever see.

Now all of that was Matt's burden because she burdened him with it, as well as his recognition that if she couldn't have Billy, if she'd ruined it with him, she'd try for Matt and in that way still have Billy.

~12~

"The sea air makes people spell bad," Billy said.

Not once since Matt had walked into Mina's did Billy's eyes break with his. He rose to greet Matt like Burt Lancaster playing Luchino Visconti's tired Leopard, and now the lovely improbability of his answer to Matt's "Spell it out for me" filled Matt with the anxiety of being lost.

Connie saluted him drunk-sailor fashion from the bar. "Cinzano," he replied with a British salute, only to turn back and find Billy still looking at him.

Billy was forty-three now.

Nah, that's not what Matt wanted to contemplate, nor the wryness of Billy's riposte, nor... maybe Billy had misunderstood, maybe he thought Matt was asking about the Florida thing, maybe he hadn't given Matt credit for sensing something more important. He turned his palms up and jerked them toward his rib cage, the impatient Sicilian command to come out with it.

Billy aged sitting there studying this privileged boy—that is how he still thought of him—whom he loved.

He took out a little yellow paper, wrote, and handed it to Matt.

Business as usual, Matt thought. Then he saw the three letters, O-U-T. He stared at the table, he listened to his blood whorl at the sink of his throat, his vision blurred, and then he did the first thing he'd ever done that announced his blood tie to Gus, he banged the table with his fist so that Connie jumped and Billy's hand instinctively slid behind his jacket.

"How d'you spell out, Billy? There's no such word. You know that? Laugh, cry, those are words. Out is a figment of your imagination. You don't get out." He paused. "Maybe you need a vacation."

That's when Billy said it, sending Matt skidding out to the edge of his being, something about the sea air and spelling bad, something that would've made Matt chuckle in any other situation.

Connie was trembling at the bar, as if the cobra had finally emerged from the council tree. She'd seen but not heard. Matt sent his gaze crashing around the room. A few savvy New Yorkers near the two men put money down and left without tallying up. But when Connie finally steadied her eyes on Billy her bemused heart steadied too, comforted as always by this frightening man. And when Matt turned back to Billy he was greeted by that same crooked, somehow innocent smile that had beguiled him years before over Herbie's soda counter. A dolphin's smile.

He got up, walked halfway to the bar and spun around and came back.

"Hey, it's too bad you never learned the language, you know that? It's *fuori di, fuori da*. Think about it, *stupido!* What're you, an astronaut, you think somebody's got a ticket for you to go to Mars? You better learn how to speak Italian."

He was hating himself for this Pieto snit but he couldn't get off it. It fascinated him. It was an archaeological dig.

"Take a walk."

Matt looked stunned: was he being dismissed, was it an invitation? Billy cocked his head toward the door and smiled.

"*Ciao*, Connie," Matt said.

"*Arrivederci*," she said with a cheer she didn't feel. She plunged a glass into the hot sink imagining Billy and Matt in White Coal, where she was born, just to distract herself. It made her laugh, the waitresses would drop things for looking sidelong at Matt, the good ole boys would shuffle too near to Billy and feel the urge to piss, or would it be the other way around? She laughed again. Hey, lookit lonesome Connie Larimer, Pa, your little gal, playing up to greasers! Maybe she'd like to take Billy to White Coal someday, not Matt though, no, Matt's too cool. Cool? I mean was ever man cooler than Billy? You know what I mean, Matt would like it but Billy'd say something real like how purely goddam mean, low and ordinary it was—damn! she was worried, scared's more like it. Fori di, fori da, what the hell'd Billy say made Matt so mad? Couldja worry about yourself, Connie, I mean couldja just worry about yourself 'steada some... she burst out bawling. Billy Salviati had never treated her with anything but respect and kindness and who else in her life could she say that for? All the boneyard donkeys who tried to feel her up in White Coal, all her horny uncles and cousins, all the whacked out musicians?—"none-a-you sonsabitches fit to tie his shoes!"

"Whose shoes, Connie?"

It was Ole Bill From Mulberry Hill/Never Worked and Never Will, Billy's favorite drunk. "Gotta a big Mister Daniels here for you, Mulberry, courtesy of Mister Billy."

"Whose shoes, Connie?"

"Oh, I was just reminiscing, Mulberry."

"Uh, I wouldn't do that if I was you, Connie. Bad for your liver, y'know, can't process it."

"Got that right," she patted the geezer's cheek.

Perhaps it would have been better for her health to know that Matt Pieto, with much more of Billy's past in his head, had similar feelings about his friend as they walked up Fifth.

"D'I ever tell you how Gran John came over here? He was a great student over there. Really. They gave him this academic medal and when he was in this procession on the way to take his first vows to study for the priesthood this monsignor rips the medal off his neck and says, You vain little rube, you're gonna start learning the humility of Our Lord Jesus Christ right now! In front of all these people. So Gran

John's walking along with tears in his eyes and he passes his uncles and this uncle says, Hey, come over here, and he goes over to his uncle and his uncle puts his arm around him and says to the monsignor, You can't have him because you don't know a good person from a bad person. So that's how Gran John joins the blessed company of all faithful people, get my drift?"

They laughed, Billy at least partly in appreciation of Matt's subtlety.

"Yeah, and then when Gran John tells me this story he says, I said to my uncle, I don't see where Jesus was so humble, and my uncle says, Giovanni, what do you see when the monsignor opens his mouth? Gran John doesn't know, so he shrugs, and his uncle sticks his two fingers in Gran's face, you know, like a forked tongue, and Gran starts laughing with tears all over his face, and that's how Gran came to America."

Billy was skiing along looking at the points of his shoes and grinning. These were the best moments of his life, listening to stories about Gran John. He reached down and massaged the back of Matthew's head.

Billy's stride was longer, looser than usual. Matt had trouble keeping up.

At Hettie's Billy made espresso, with lemon twists. The gentility of this gesture moved Matt back into the psychic space he'd occupied listening to Gran John speak of Woozy Lomento. Matt had known Hettie, of course, but it had never occurred to him that Billy might be living here.

He noticed changes in the place. Everywhere books were open, marked with ribbons, news clippings, dried leaves. "You read these?" Matt swept his upturned palm around the walls of books.

Billy looked pained. "Yeah, some."

Gray's Manual of Botany, Frances Yates, Evelyn Underhill... Woozy Lomento... he remembered staring at Gran's tomatoes. "I don't know what to say."

"That's new."

Discretion and politesse, qualities that made him valuable to his grandfathers, he jettisoned as if his life depended on it.

"Billy, please don't misunderstand me, I really need to know—how'd you, you know, how'd you do it?"

"You mean the big words? What's the big deal? You just read the dictionary till your head starts squeakin', then you read it some more, an' you keep on readin' it every time you read anythin' else, an' after a while you're a genius."

"So how come you still talk t'me like a dude? I thought we were friends."

Billy was stung. He took a long time answering.

"Geez, Matt, I didn't mean, you know, to condescend to you or anything, but I didn't figure I had a right to change the deal."

"The deal? You mean it would be like finessing a card?"

"Yeah."

Fragments of Yeats perned in the gyre of his head. The center would not hold, the ordered center of his life, upon which he bitterly and sometimes resentfully depended, was breaking up.

John had ordered a bad, some would say dumb thing out of the pain of a wound that had never stopped festering. Billy had done it. And now they were no longer the men they had promised John they would always be. In the heart of loyalty he felt betrayed and expressed it in a silly way. "But how'd you figure out how to say the words?"

"I dunno. Radio, television. Christ, what's so hard about it? I don't say 'em all right, but who'd'ya think I'm talkin' to every day, Anthony Eden?"

"I didn't think you hardly talked to anybody."

"I talked to Hettie."

"I'm sorry, Billy."

"Sorry sucks, I don' want you should be sorry, Matt, I want you should help me."

A map of the Mediterranean was spread on a coffee table, a small Cycladic head holding it down on one end, a green bud vase inlaid with silver at the other end. Malta, Sardinia, Tangiers and Taormina in Sicily were circled in red. A black felucca with red sails, a Saracen boat, plied the air on a fake stone plinth by the window. Billy sat next to the felucca in a Savonarola field chair watching Matt walking around, fingering Hettie's—he could not settle on the right word—mementos, totems. Then he spotted a rice paper scroll about four feet long embedded between bookcases. The elongated black letters looked as if they had been painted on rapidly as with Zen calligraphy. What they lacked in Kufic formality they more than made up in certitude. He was about to move on when he recognized that this was English script.

"The trinity is this: the krater, my hands over it, and the *prima materia* flowing through them."

Matt felt the agony of Giordano Bruno burning at the stake. He felt cold rivulets behind his ears. These were not sensibilities he could share with Billy. He writhed in this dilemma until he realized these were Billy's sensibilities.

"You wrote this?"

Billy went to the door and beckoned like a Sforza count. They went up to the roof. Matt had the sensation of floating. They moved like strangers in a gallery. Billy looked so casually under the leaves of Hettie's roses for aphids and mites that Matt envisioned him having done so for years on end.

"The landlord was worried about the roof. I told him he'd worry less if he sold it to us. Then I reinforced it."

"Us." The word made Matt homesick.

"When I get up in the morning I sit on the bed for a minute, then I make the sign of the cross so it should be a good day, I go to the bathroom, I get out my shaving stuff and who do I see? Matthew Pieto, he's still there, Gran John's boy. You, you wanna look in the mirror some morning and see some other guy. Who do you see, Billy, tell me?"

"Some sad paisano. I think his name is Lorenzo di Credi."

Matt spewed his espresso like a stone frog into a tub of roses. He turned around to see Billy smiling a smile much too big for his narrow face. He was incredulous. The next time the two of them looked at each other they were shaking with laughter. Billy had filched a little file marked amusement right out of his friend's memory. He'd been meaning to tell Billy for several years that he looked like the Renaissance artist di Credi's self-portrait. Billy took small pruning shears from a box seat, cut out a Chicago Beauty and passed the petiole through an eyelet of Matt's lapel, like a big brother sprucing him up for confirmation.

"If you spell it out for your grandfather, he'll hear it."

A timer flicked on an arcade of fairy lights. Quarter to ten. Matt noticed a glass enclosure to the rear. Billy left for more espresso and when he returned he found Matt, looking charred, sitting under a ficus among patinaed replicate statuary. He had never shown Billy the magical celestial engine painted on the vaulted ceiling of his bedroom by his friend Paolo Maio; now Billy had shared all this, and he felt ashamed.

~13~

"You think that big son of a bitch's smarter'n I think 'e is?"

"He had a pretty good question, Grandpa."

Gus Pieto looked fondly on Santo's son, unable as always to fathom how so fine a thing had come of disappointment and madness. Maria Altobene had much to do with it, he knew, and for this she had his unswerving respect.

They had been talking of Billy's business trip to Florida when Joey Carbone, who had access to Gus' baser side, said, "How'd 'e do that, Boss, how'd 'e know 'e'd go take a dump on da boat?"

Maria flipped a spoonful of ricotta onto his nose.

"Watch you mouth!" Gus said, and Joey ducked out the door with an apologetic look at Maria.

"So how'd 'e do that, Matthew? That Billy's a card."

"Ask him."

"I can't ask him. He don't belong to me. I'm askin' you."

"It's what he does. He knows how to do things."

"He's the saddest guy I ever knew."

"You...."

"Care? No, Matteo, I let you care."

The old erect bear squeezed John's arm, kissed his daughter-in-law's forehead, pinched Matt's cheek, and left.

Once Gus was gone he was, in respect, never mentioned.

"About Billy," Matt started. John's hands froze with a peat-boxed tomato transplant in them. Maria twisted her apron. "He needs something."

"So give it to him." John resumed his task.

But Maria stood still.

"I can't, it's up to you."

"What is it you can't do, Matteo?"

"Could you sit down, Gran, we really gotta talk."

"Whuh, he wants to be me?"

"Papa," Maria slammed a plate on the drainboard, "when you say something, no matter how silly it is, Matthew listens. I listen."

"No man could have a better daughter," Gran John said, studying the fixity of Maria's stare.

"So?"

"So, I listen."

He sat down, laced his fingers, and looked at his grandson. Maria busied herself again.

"Billy wants out."

Maria dropped her knife in the sink.

"I think we'll have a little glass of Corvo," John said.

Matt nodded. Maria brought three glasses, signifying she wanted in. John poured like a celebrant.

"Don't ask me what I said, I said what you would say."

"An'?"

"He said to ask you."

Maria had her left hand at her throat, she was looking at her son, then her eyes slid around to John and stopped.

"That's your mother's don't-make-a-speech look." Matthew knew it well. From Maria came his silences.

"Everything you ever asked him, Gran, he's done."

"If I can't make a speech, what can I say?"

"He's..."

"He's what?" John threw out his open palm.

"A certain kind of dead."

"I only know one kind of dead. If you know another kind of dead, Matteo, maybe you listen too much to those priests."

Now Maria's gaze fell. The room felt dark. "There are many kinds of dead, Papa."

John got up and walked to the window overlooking his roof garden. He spun around as a young button in a dark alley would.

"Hey! My name is John Altobene. I put the bread on your table, I gotta shut my mouth? Do I look like, like Santa Claus, ho ho ho? Lissen t'me, both 'a you. You talk t'me about some kind of dead like I'm somebody's stupid old uncle. I knew more about dead before you was born than you'll ever know. Who d'you think pays for you to sit on your asses and tell me there are things too refined for me to understand? Refined? I know refined. Refined's an excuse for no heart, no guts. You think I don' understand diff'ren' kindsa dead, Maria? Huh? I'll tell you somethin' about dead, dead is what I'm gonna be soon, an' what're you gonna be? Heh? You gonna be me, Matteo? I don't think so, do you, Maria?"

His daughter's eyes were wide open and respectful. This was her real father, the one her son barely knew, the one she loved and feared.

"So who? Gus? You see the veins on his hands? I'm gonna live to throw dirt on him. Then what? You got a college education, Matteo, you tell me. Hey, your mother, she got a college education, we ask her. Maria, then what? I'll tell you what. Billy can be any kind of dead except stinking with the flies in the Meadowlands, because when I go Billy is what you got. You, Matteo. An' don' gimme that look, don' gimme any look, because you know what I'm talking about, I'm talking about stones, which you don' got."

"You didn't bring him up to have them, Papa."

"You right. Somebody shoulda brought me up not to have them. So whud am I gonna do? You wanna be God, Matteo, you better open your eyes a little bit."

Maria's chin quarreled with her father.

"Yeah, that's right, the Lord giveth and the Lord taketh. Matteo gives me Billy, now he wants to take him, so if he wants to play God he better act like God. God sees the consequences of what He does. Hey, who am I? That's what the priests say, right? Billy Salviati, best soldier in the army, my army. Only boy I ever knew scare the hell outta me. Thank God, he's your friend. Tell him I bless him."

Matthew went slack in relief.

"He's tired. He should be tired, he done a lotta work, I oughtta know. He needs a vacation."

Matthew jerked up again. Maria shook her head like a mare with fleas.

The two men had exhausted each other. They looked to Maria for help. What she thought she would not share, that there are no more Billies. One generation, that's all. The grand old men, Maranzano; the new order, Lucana; the throwbacks, Pieto, Altobene; the mechanics, Nicky d'Alessio, Billy.

"I don't know," Matthew said in frustration.

"You better know, Matteo. Blood ain't Pellegrino, y'know. You better figure this out."

Even after Gran John had gone down into the cellar Matthew felt the old man's finger pointing at him. They heard him moving things.

Maria looked at him from under a lowering brow.

"I don't know."

"I don't think you heard him, Matthew, he said you better figure this out."

He looked at his mother with his left hand tucked under his right elbow, a fist at his mouth.

She had loved this pose since she first saw him strike it as a teenager trying out various roles, suits of armor.

"You, Matteo, you figure it out. See?"

"Si, Mama."

They smiled.

John came up from the cellar. He too was smiling. He had a large puppet dangling from a Greek cross. "The Saraceno." He manipulated the Saracen knight's strings menacingly. "Your great grandfather, he made the Saraceno. The Saraceno, what does he fear?"

"The Knights of Malta," Matthew said, glad for a break in the heaviness.

"Nah! He eats them for antipasto."

"What then?"

"I dunno. Ask your friend Billy. But I tell you what I fear. All the dumb bastards in this world don' know which end is up, the empty suits, big shots with their heads up their asses makin' problems outta yes 'n no, 'cause when we give the world to them we gonna hope to God Christ never come back here to be so disgusted. He gonna look at those fairies in his church and he gonna kick their asses like he done before, I swear to God. Here, you give this to Billy, tell him take a year, take two years while his friend Matteo grows up. Take it to him." He shook the Saraceno's strings. "Yeah, this is him. In a few days I'm gonna give you money for him, plenty, don' worry, okay?"

His mother nodded inside his peripheral view. He took the puppet, kissed the old man—"You need a shave, Gran"—and left.

It never occurred to Billy that by luck he found Matthew Pieto, by luck he made himself useful to John Altobene. If it had been luck—he had Schwartzbear's word for this—he'd have bad breath.

Nothing since Schwartzbear fled Dannemora on a stretcher, since Billy said so long to Franklin Jones, since he'd met Hettie Warshaw, had changed that. If anything, Hettie taught him in a more formal way than he'd known before how to make his own luck.

Billy observed Matt's agonizing, bemused and compassionate. It was a luxury he could never afford. He examined it like King Kong sniffing Fay Wray. It must be good. It must be aristocratic, something it would be nice to have. But he didn't, and that was that. And he didn't know that it was his own directitude that attracted Matt Pieto.

Psychotic it may be, but when you're born to pure damned luck and it keeps raining down on you, sun-struck and dazzling with love and approval, you might in this fortunate despair envy a man like Billy Salviati, especially if he happened to love you.

Matt already had achieved his one ambition, one so modest he was ashamed to own up to it. Billy, that stone executioner, had shown him his heart. If he had wished it, he would have shown him all the lethal uses of C3, his skills, his arsenal. And to Billy he'd shown nothing.

Years ago he'd commissioned his friend Paolo Maio to paint the stars in their courses on his bedroom ceiling so that he might go about his business with their grandeur on his mind.

He got this idea from the Frances Yates biography of Giordano Bruno. The magus and visionary, burned at the stake as a heretic for summoning the powers of star demons, was just the ticket for a man who'd recently quit seminary.

As Paolo charted and vaulted the heavens of Matt's birth night the two men shared dinners on dropcloths, sitting like Arabs at their fires. Matt planned these meals exactingly, choosing a new wine each evening. He wanted Paolo to feel like a favored Renaissance artist. Paolo, a tall man elongated like an El Greco, sat cross-legged reading the Yates biography between stints on the ladder.

Matt suggested recessing pinpricks of light for the major stars, but after two weeks Paolo rebelled. The idea, he said, is rank fatalism, like drawing dot to dot. Live your life by dead reckoning, what a waste! He wouldn't do it. It was like sentencing a friend to be a prisoner at large. No, a sentient man's heavens must be filled with novas, comets, quasars, the jubilant creativity of the cosmos. Matthew listened carefully, then acceded with a smiling sweep of his head, at first thinking he'd offended his friend by asking him to do a pedestrian thing, then slowly recognizing that Paolo wanted to design a celestial engine for him, and, finally, that Paolo had apprehended Bruno's intent.

They spoke of Bruno in the courts of Catherine de Medici and Elizabeth. Matt said that Bruno's auto-da-fe in 1600 ushered in the scientific age. He told Paolo how he'd discovered Bruno in two worn green volumes in an antiquarian bookstore on lower Broadway.

"It was as if I had a dowsing rod in my hands, I just walked all the way to the back and my hands pulled me to Bruno."

Paolo tossed back a pale forelock. To Matt he looked like a Lombard prince.

"You know, the church burned the two men Elizabeth thought most highly of, Cranmer and Bruno, Cranmer at the beginning of her life and Bruno at the end. She was pissed about Cranmer, but I wonder what thoughts were in that wily old henna head about Bruno."

As he spoke he rose, climbed a ladder and was picking at a fiery star with his forefinger when Matt said, "I imagine it saddened her, it must have felt part of her old age, something that wouldn't have happened earlier, something like God one by one taking things from her."

He stared down at a ramekin of caponata, then sent his grave green gaze up to his friend.

"I doubt the church—our church, Paolo—burned Cranmer for his heresies. I think they burned him for putting them so damned well."

Paolo ran his elegant hand through his hair.

"Matteo, Matteo, a good poem haunts your mind. You know, ...*will pardon Paul Claudel / pardons him for writing well?* Auden's *In Memory of W. B. Yeats*? You know the Episcopalians chucked Cranmer's prayer book."

"Yeah, I guess they no longer felt deserving. Once in a while I drop in on this perverse little St. Hilda's that still uses the old book and I can hear the English back then saying, 'Yeah man, give us the light and the way!' Cranmer made the

Latin sound like hocus-pocus. England finally contracted the Renaissance and language was the virus."

"Oh, be not so hard on poor old Rome, Matteo. After all, it did inspire the Renaissance."

"Nay Paolo, what a misguided thing for an artist to say! There was a renaissance in spite of the church. We owe it to the princes, not the popes."

Paolo was silent. He deemed Matthew a prince. He saw people as he would sculpt them, as the material he'd use. He saw his friend's face worn by torrents of other people's regard into a series of catenaries: when you looked at him your gaze slid over his face like water until you reached his eyes, and only later you might note the soft brown hair, the Etruscan shoulders and lion's gait. Burgundian limestone, he decided, roseate, secret.

<h1 style="text-align:center">~14~</h1>

P

People need to talk to Matt when they see him. It's urgent. This and his parents' surname make him mythic, his means unrelated to his work. His work is a little of this and a little of that. His life, as the Sufis say, is his work, but it's not evident. He lives modestly but well. It might be said he's a courier. His nature shapes the messages he bears.

His handsomeness is so understated that men take no offense. Women wonder what to want of him and rarely decide. It is that quality that worries Maria—perhaps the right woman will always elude him, or he will elude her.

Men weary of ambush and women of black bless him. A treaty between murdering clans, Gran John said when he saw him, "Let me kiss an angel." Santo's father, the fearfully scarred Gus, leaned over solemnly and pronounced, "I bless you, my grandson."

The child was born aware of duty. From the crib he divided his attentions like a cardinal. He was burdened from birth by Maria's inability to conceive again.

What finally bound the pensive John Altobene and the brutal Gus Pieto was not the improbable marriage of their children but their mutual pity and dismay: Santo was mad and the old men had their hands full keeping him from braining his family.

The grotesque masque of her most recent beating was fading from Maria's lovely face and Matthew was recovering from a mild concussion when the gift that fixed his stars took its first bow. Like deer taking sanctuary by a reservoir, they had fled to John's darkly fitted brownstone on Nineteenth Street. Gus had come by to see his grandson. Maria read his stare well. Pity and contempt. Why would a beautiful woman if she had any brains at all marry Santo? He shook his head like a lion with gnats in its eyes.

Matt was seated on a piano stool leafing through a book of Renaissance art. He was eleven. His adult life was about to begin.

"So show me the picture you like best, Matteo," John said. In a hushed movement the boy rose, came to his grand-father's chair and showed him Michelangelo's *Pieta*. The old man stared at God dead in his mother's arms. He stared into the boy's certain eyes. The long scar under his right jaw blanched. The tick of the wind-up clock on the mantel rattled the house. Gus, who boasted he could see around corners, sensed advent. He quit the silver whiskey tray by the window and stood behind John's right shoulder. John looked up at his old enemy and pointed to the picture.

"Ahhh Christ," Gus sighed.

In a month Santo was in Sicily where nobody figured he'd grow old, and the old men's truce became an armistice.

The boy's fortunateness redoubled. His usefulness began. The old men got that way judging character well and they saw that their grandson knew how to deliver a message.

A lupine Santo, *lupara* draped over his arm, eyes moon-swarmed, ranging stony Sicily gradually supplanted in his son's mind the images that exiled him there. He began to take wrong turns, stumbling onto film-negative dimensions stunned with sheet-metal thunder and heat lightning, unbalanced by the knowledge that this awful father's fate was sealed the very moment his son's gift to sway men innocently appeared.

He had what chroniclers said of Alexander the Great, *perpetua fortuno*. Possessed by it. The Macedonian conqueror, half in irony, half in wonder, declared himself a god and pressed his godly kin to the edge of their tolerance.

But Matt's luck vexed him. No strange mother had promised it him. When he disowned it he was dismayed to see it grow. He had never heard Billy say luck has bad breath, but if he had he would have embraced the idea.

Where others, deprived of love, wreck their lives insisting on their due, Matt drowned in love. He went to seminary to deserve it, learned it's undeserved, and quit.

His mind could not keep its course, its compass swung to magnetic distractions. To find true north required true references. All Matteo's references were fey.

Paolo, when he was finished building Matt's engine, went home to Baltimore for a friend's gallery opening, leaving his paints and brushes and tools behind. He never called for them. Matt had to ship them. He had intuited enough of Matt's life to know that this engine was built for a purpose, not a lark, not a whim. He needed by the time he left to contemplate his friend from afar. In a word, having neither seen nor heard anything overt, he was frightened. Good. It was good. Where Matt's true life was concerned Paolo Maio's ignorance was his armor.

Nobody sane threatened the life of the grandchild of John Altobene and Gus Pieto, but nonetheless Matt knew his life hung today on his chances of steadying the yaw of his mind.

This was no errand. It wasn't a mission either. It was the second time Billy asked him to grow up. Not an invitation but a demand. First in Patsy's pizzeria. That opened the bracket. Now Billy was asking him to close the bracket, to parenthesize his entire adult life inside, and set out looking for harm.

Gran John understood him. He knew what he was asking, even if Gran John deliberately misinterpreted it. Matthew had his answer. Billy had his answer. All the courier had to do was deliver it. Deliver it and go on his lucky way. What the hell, Billy had been lucky enough. Nobody owed him, nobody in the Pieto or Altobene families anyway.

Lover of art, he saw his predicament as the light of heaven. Maria to his left, the dogs of hell to his right. Lifelong he'd leftward veered, but only because hell so far conjured no siren.

The only pressing business on his schedule today was to sell a six-story tenement on Baxter Street owned by Frank Turco, or, better, held in trust by Frank Turco.

"I'm gonna sell it for a million five, Frankie," he told The Turk on the phone, "a million two for you and the rest for the church, *capiche?* Yeah, I'm gonna sell it to some Chinks from Hong Kong or maybe some Egyptians."

"Whatsamatter, Italians broke?"

"Hey Frankie, Italians sell, Chinks buy, got it?"

Matt spoke three languages, two of them English: the profane interrogative of the Manhattan streets, the speech of his prep school and college, and Sicilian. He enjoyed gutter patois. He was creative.

"Chinks're buyin' Little Italy, I don' wanna sell to no Chinks, Matt."

"You *stupido!* Whuh, d'I ask you?"

Just what Gus, chucking his head up, would've said. Matt had patience. These little contretemps amused him. It was theater.

"Hey, they can have Little Italy, they can have Big Italy, if they pay for it, but I think we gonna keep Sicily, awright Frankie? Jus' to remind us how far we come." He tried to humor him.

"Yeah, okay, Mattie, jes' between us rock farmers, right?"

Matt gave the handset a comical look. He knew the dumb jerk was standing at the other end already smelling the cash in a bag. Feeding an Elizabeth Street primate first thing in the morning was not his idea of a great way to start the day, but the grandfathers counted on him for such tasks.

"I look like a sar... a sar what, Mattie? Come on, Mattie, tell me." This was the ritual when Frank needed to be reassured Matthew wasn't mad at him. None of them had ever seen Matthew angry, but they all assumed it could be fatal.

"A sarcophagus, Frank," he said for the thousandth time since the big janissary fell down drunk at his feet one hot August night and Matt, a wannabe Jesuit building a vocabulary, told him when he woke that he looked like a sarcophagus.

Now whenever he thought of Matt he thought of the sar-what. Indeed he'd told a number of impressed doxies he looked like a sarcophagus.

Age made John philosophical, Gus irascible, and in any case Matthew was in many ways the man they would have liked to be. It wasn't a flaw to them that he couldn't do what they'd done, wouldn't, was not that vulgar. Matt perceived this and it saddened him because he did not wish either beloved man to fault himself.

The sun was scrubbing his apartment white by the time he left and walked west on East Sixty-Fourth. He was closing in on what he thought was the truth of Giordano Bruno's ilk, Ficino and the other alchemists, that the gold they sought of lesser metals was really the transmutation of the human mettle to realize God operative in every ion of creation. This, not his espousal of Galileo and Copernicus, was why the inquisitors killed Bruno. A prayerful human is God's co-operator of the universe. Call down the star beasts and demons for good things, Bruno said. Yeah, the perfectibility of man, that's what stuck in those priestly craws, that and the notion we're all priests.

So, set right by Paolo the astrocartographer and Bruno the imaginator, Matteo headed for Washington to get his bearings before he became a hostage in Passaic or some like ill befell him while he was arguing with the gods about their unfathomable generosity.

But first, as those very gods would have it, he had to encounter Violet and Roy Cosgrove.

The Cosgroves were one of the ways he spit in the palm of fortune. Roy had been a playwright, Violet an actress. Booze-wrecked in their forties, they could be grand and endearing sober. Their British accents (how many accents that dotty, verbally savage little island spoke) helped them cadge drinks, mostly from younger not-quite-so-ruined drunks. They'd been something, done something, but the gods had bothered to give them a fatal thirst, or was it a gene, while on Matthew they'd strewn casual abundance and sense. It irked him. Irksomeness was as close to Santo's door as he came.

When Matt thought of Bruno he could think of God, but when he considered the whimsicality of things he thought of gods; why not both?

"Caro Matteo," Violet cried, "let me kiss you, darling!"

Her kisses were welcome when she was sober.

"Good to see you, old son," Roy said. A firm hand and a good gray gaze.

"You two are psychic. You've been on my mind, I want to invite you to dinner tomorrow night."

"Yes?" said Roy warily.

"But there's a caveat."

Roy looked vindicated. The Cosgroves waited apprehensively; drunks are defenseless against such trepidations.

"I want you to come early, say five. Be sober. I have something wonderful to show you."

Five was the last hour he could hope to see the Cosgroves sober. Dinner was secondary. He couldn't bear to give them money on the street, so he'd slip it into their coats at dinner, as he'd done so often.

As he took in their childish delight at a civilized invitation, as if they were again what they'd been, Matthew recognized that he'd decided something important: they would be first to see his firmament. He didn't know why, but he knew such impulses changed people's lives. Almost any change in theirs would be welcome. Perhaps Paolo's engine could bear them somewhere good.

"*Ciao*, darling," and Violet blew him a kiss as if she were again beautiful and innocent. Roy winked generously. Plucky in destitution. Matt liked them very much, indeed admired them. Try to stay alive for such people, he told himself.

He was the Hermes of subterranean gods at war. He knew where to put his feet, what to say, and how to look. But was it a proper calling? What is proper? The good he did was soiled by circumstance. He'd had a dream from which somehow he'd made out that he should go to seminary, be a priest.

He stood on a causeway. It was white and gold. Behind were lakes and poplars, calm and certain. Tuscany, Paolo said. Before him roiled a sea of blood. He took the lakes and forests for his grandfathers, the sea he took for Santo, priestliness seemed the alternative. He was not unaware that his grandfathers had, surgeon-like, washed blood from their hands in ghastly sinks in Newark and Jersey City, but what he had experienced of them was love. These speculations were the thorns and snares of his life, they filled him like Muzak in elevators until he was wild to get off. But he couldn't. He had been sending himself these invitations to a crucifixion since he was eleven.

Now, strolling towards Penn Station, he recalled John's daft solution.

"Matteo, you gotta marry a nice Italian girl, like Josefina."

"I don't like Italian girls, Granpa."

"Did I say like, did I say love, whuddid I say? I said you marry one. You want blondes, you can have blondes. You want redheads, you can have redheads, but a nice Italian girl is gonna give you..." Granpa John, looking pleadingly for the felicitous phrase, weighed it in both hands.

"Is gonna give me *bambini*, right?"

"So? I thought you didn't wanna be a priest no more. What's wrong with babies, is a law against it now?"

"Nothing, Granpa, even you were a baby once."

"No, Matteo, I was never a baby. I was born old, I swear to God. My mother looked at me and she say, He's gonna take good care of me. My papa looked at me and he say, Jesus Christ!"

Matteo laughed. "What did he say Jesus Christ for?"

The old man shook out his right hand like a rag, the Sicilian hand sign for anything so hot or horrible words cannot serve it, the sort of gesture, if it concerned one's sister, one killed for.

"What did your sisters and brothers say?" Matt asked, enjoying himself.

"They said, Lookit him, he's a mule, we gonna ride him to church."

Matt smiled so broadly his teeth showed. The old man beamed.

"I know you're not a fairy, so whatsamatter with you? I see you with this nice girl, that nice girl, maybe not an Italian girl, but I make her a nice meal anyway and she disappear. Whuddya do to them, Matteo?"

"I dunno, Grandpa. One thing I don't do is scare the hell out of them."

"So what is that supposed to mean, Mr. College Man, huh?"

"I'm sorry, Granpa, just being a smart-ass."

"Matteo my friend, one big thing I like about you is you not a smart-ass, but you don' enjoy like you should. You read too much maybe. Me, I eat this, I drink that, I smoke a Parodi, I sing, I eat life, you know what I'm saying? Tell you what, maybe you should scare hell outta them sometime, girls I think they like that."

Matt laughed again. They embraced happily.

John blew a long foul line of stogie smoke before making the ultimate concession to manly love. "I tell you what, you wanna bring a nice blonde with a nose like a razor blade home to your grandfather I'm gonna make a Sicilian girl out of her."

"Granpa, not even Italian girls are Sicilian, just the men."

His grandfather looked at him like an inquiring dog. "You say something good? Yeah, maybe I think you right. Jesus Haych Christ, Matteo, if the goddam women was Sicilian!" He shook his hand out violently.

"Get outta here!" Matt cried, and they laughed.

"So what's Gus gonna do with this nice blonde, Granpa?"

John chuckled. He loved being fed such lines. "He gonna scare the hell outta her for you."

John didn't know about Matt's fulfilled ambition, and if he did he still wouldn't have guessed that it might not be a lover to whom Matteo would show it first, and one thing more he didn't know that would have explained the emptiness he saw in his grandson: no woman had ever hurt Matt because no woman's going had ever left him with less than he'd had. He never confused his charmed life with a woman. He was clear that if his life had a talisman it wasn't a woman. He didn't know what it was to feel bereft, but he knew with foreboding that he would know when John or Gus died. Matt wasn't the sort of man women hurt because he didn't make a good witness to meanness or shenanigans. All he knew of love was what he felt for Maria and John and Gus.

"When I knock on your door a stranger answers," his friend, briefly his lover, Robin Ayling, had said to him. He'd grown up a man's man, not a woman's pawn. Maria had never assumed mythological proportions to him the way some men's mothers do when the men in their lives orbit around them. Maria was John's daughter. John was sun, center, authority, and vision. That Maria failed to become a person in her own right eluded the men. Since Santo's departure—he vanished without a rumor—no one had seen Maria eyeing a man, until Matthew watched her and Billy, and her men acted as if they knew why, but they didn't. She was frightened, and among such men she didn't have to do anything about it.

Neither tall nor short, no jock, a player of jai alai with near professionalism, usually content with squash, Matt never felt competitive. In a messenger that's good.

~15~

Blasted tenements, upended half-buried bathtub madonnas, cubes of flattened cars, dry squalls of windows and wretched laundry preoccupied Matt from Elizabeth to Wilmington as his train lurched and retched. What's going on behind the windows? he wondered. If a man could imagine being invisible there must be invisible beings, a world that could only be caught sidelong for a second.

He remembered now what he'd so liked in the writings of the Afghan Idries Shah, that the object of the Sufi is to become invisible. Yeah, he smiled. Dirty lace curtains blowing in moldy windows of river towns moved him. He thought of the tumid Chemung staining Elmira, the prison town haunted by Confederate dead, that he visited on occasion to brief certain paisani and assure them they had not been forgotten. He wanted to hear the stories of those beer-bellies on the stoops of their august upstate towns, and the stories of thin girls pushing carriages across the blazing street from adolescence to old age.

But if he really wanted to hear their stories he'd get off and start walking, right? Maybe. Perhaps he would.

Matt Pieto, when his classmates remembered him, was re-membered for how remarkably innocent he was of the need to speak. And, depending on who you were, you re-membered first what a profound listener he was or how silent he was. Your pick, and it marked you.

He blanked the muse of dilapidation by opening *The Times*. A drawing on the op-ed page attracted him, he found it reassuring. It accompanied a think piece about another of California's notorious taxation schemes. Two young people, art deco gargoyles really, right-angled like bridge abutments to support a Malibu house deck on which an elderly man and woman disported themselves obscenely: the young taxed for the old. Neither the drawing nor its message interested him, but the drawing faced left toward the story's headline and the Pacific. It was given that the Pacific was out there on the left, as if the reader bore the map of North America in mind. Matt felt part of the community of people who notice and are reassured by such things, like being a familiar communicant at low Mass.

The hurtling train lulled him into reverie. He thought of the sea, of stars and Giordano Bruno, and of an old man who seemed once years before to have stepped out of a Titian at The National Gallery of Art, his destination today.

It's one thing, he thought, for a sailor to know how to shoot the sun or one of the fifty or so navigational stars, it's another thing for the sea to give him a steady enough deck to do it.

Bruno believed star demons bestir themselves on behalf of those who can summon them. What could have unsettled the bowels of the ecclesiastics about this notion, smacking as it did of the Apocalypse, unless they suspected it to be true?

The night sky of his birth would remain nothing more than myth and bestiary unless he could unlock its powers. And if he could, what is it that Matthew Pieto would? Something about love, but all the legions of Macedon were at the frontiers of his mind beating back that barbarian thought. And if it were love, love for whom? He knew the answer would ambush him.

Sea, sea green, Titian green: he remembered the Spanish grandee who'd stepped from a wide-angle Titian court scene and followed him at a respectful remove from gallery to gallery until they stood before a Corot, *Ville d'Avray*, where the old man with the goatee spoke. "Do you know why it holds your attention, young sir?"

Its serenity, Matthew was about to say, when the delicate little man smiled.

Am I talking to a ghost, Matthew had wondered. He looked around to see if other eyes would confirm the man's existence. Then slowly he too smiled.

"You are a much older man than I am, my friend."

Matthew nodded sadly.

"Do you know..."

His face quizzed the grandee.

"...why it holds your attention?"

Matthew smiled again.

"It's because he painted it in the crack."

Matthew's lips parted. He strained to understand, and he thought he understood, then it eluded him. He stared into the old man's extraordinarily young black eyes.

"Yes, yes, the crack. You're like a crowbar, you are a crowbar, and you slip into the hole, and you twist this way and that way, and then you feel it give way, it opens and you go in. But do you? Go in? Maybe. You would, my boy, you would."

He stood letting Matthew's gaze rise and ebb over his face.

Matthew lowered his head, thinking, then looked up into the man's eyes and furrowed his brow. But the grandee said no more. Abruptly he turned and walked off. Then he wheeled, shook his forefinger at Matt and said, "You have to learn how to live in the crack."

And was that now why he was going to Washington, to prize open the crack, to ransack it for himself, for Billy?

The little painting's silvery susurrations—the aspen leaves were to him an angelus—were his religion. Alexander had entrails. Matthew had Corot. If he could end his quarrel—or even make a truce—with his luck, it might be in *Ville d'Avray*, in Papa Corot's eye. By that pond, in that leaf-swept, exquisite moment in the fullness of a season, he might consent to all his grandfathers had given him. The terrible underwater chiming of *omerta* might be transcribed to the sigh of aspen.

Sailors used to cast coins in Alexander's image to propitiate demons in the sea. Seminary was the least likely place for Matthew to learn that more than a few people felt that way about him. Alexander may have shared some of his luck with sailors and Roman admirers, but Matthew offered *deja vu*, a sense of having come from somewhere else and better. He seemed to say, We're not from here and we have only to bear this place a little while. How could a man riven at his core bestow such benignity? He didn't know any more than he knew how murderers love.

He'd asked by phone from New York if *Ville d'Avray* were hanging, asked with such pleasant authority that someone in that great institution troubled to confirm that it was and felt rewarded for troubling.

In the Impressionists' wing he felt the fingertips of someone's eyes feather the back of his head. This intrusion annoyed him. He turned to see a vivid blonde of medium height and feral demeanor across the gallery. Her smile flickered because she was unsure he'd return it. He didn't. He seized her oblique gaze and strode quickly to her as a Roman tribune might have picked someone in a crowd from whom he wished to hear.

"It won't be any news to you," he said, "that you are disturbingly beautiful, but maybe you'll like to remember someday that once in The National Gallery a stranger walked up to you and said so because he liked your smile." He paused, studying her. "Do you speak English?"

"I am French, monsieur, but I understand you very well."

"You see," Matthew continued, "I'm working on a certain problem by watching that French village over there, and this problem is very important to me."

She wrinkled her nose. After a few seconds more they smiled, she with puzzlement and a dash of amusement, he with inquiring concentration. He looked at her until he was sure she knew she'd been liked, then he returned to *Ville d'Avray*.

He'd lost a chance to end his quarrel with grace because he didn't see that this is the way he paid for it, this way of going out of his way to cross others' brows like a fair wind. As he turned from the girl he did feel loss and he knew it was not loss of opportunity to come on, but something else, something that brushed and yet eluded him. He didn't know that this manner, this willingness to say odd things at risk, was uncommon. It wasn't humility that blinded him. It was that nobody had ever wanted to break the spell by telling him.

As he moved now from figure to tree to pond to house in *Ville d'Avray* he became lost: had he come to see the painting or the girl? That it could be both escaped him. After a while they turned and found each other's eyes again. This time their eyes crinkled with humor. No one could have seen a smile on Corot's peasant woman, it wasn't that kind of painting, but Matthew did.

~16~

In the evening he was greeted on the steps of his brownstone by a nun in mufti.

Verrazano's wind cooled Manhattan's fevers and he found himself foolishly glad to see Dolly Fitzsimmons.

"I'm sorry I'm not a Medici princess, Matthew." Her wide, friendly face frowned comically.

"Perhaps you were Catherine in another life."

"I hope not. What would I have to look forward to? Surely not to being a li'l ole American nun. Besides, you know the church doesn't believe in reincarnation."

"I'm very glad to see you."

To embrace seemed the thing to do, but....

"Dear Matthew, it's so like you to ignore cues. Most other men would've said the church didn't believe the earth was round either."

He leaned on the iron balustrade waiting for their banter to subside, their business to begin.

"I'm in the throes of a crisis, Matt, and I had this compulsion to see you."

"How long've you been sitting here?"

"A while. I had no otherwhere to go."

He smiled, liking her "otherwhere."

"I've been to Washington to see a painting."

Dolly's face lit with glee. "Oh Matt, I suppose you had nothing in the world better to do!"

"I hadn't."

"Other men go to Washington to plead cases, press causes, testify or be crowned with laurel."

He looked at Dolly with the eyeless gaze of a Greek statue.

She smiled through pursed lips, cast her eyes downward for a time and said finally, "Hermes Tresmegistus, most blessed messenger of the gods."

He looked at the sun razing acrid Jersey.

"The gods may not be who you think they are, Dolly."

"Well, that's all right, dear heart, I don't believe in them anyway, I can't, can I? That's partly what I want to talk to you about. What I can believe, I mean."

"Everything. I'll listen to everything, Dolly."

"And will you let me do that for you, Matthew?"

"Do I look as if I have something to say?"

"It's the strangest thing in a messenger, you never look as if you have anything to say. Yet I know you're troubled. As much as you love art you'd not have gone to Washington to see a painting unless you needed advice."

This insight pleased him. But then he remembered she'd called him a messenger, not that she was wrong. "So what makes you think I'm a messenger?"

"You told me in an unguarded moment that you delivered messages for your grandfathers. Then they came to visit you at school and I saw them, so I figured you weren't riding a bicycle around Manhattan toppling old ladies for tips."

He searched: apparently he'd confided in this woman: what had he been feeling for her then?

"D'you remember what a scandal you caused when you said in seminary it's too bad nuns couldn't hear confessions because they listened better than priests? You passionate mariologist! I've wondered if that was your subtle way of flirting with me."

"It was." He remembered now there'd been other nuns in that class.

"What devil sent you the White Goddess instead of the dark night of the soul, Matthew?"

"A she-devil, of course. I have an imaginary sister, she's younger than me and a lot smarter."

"What's her name?"

"Dolores."

"I'm not sure I'm happy to hear that. I may be wrong, Matt, but I think it's unusual to have an imaginary confidante of the opposite sex." Her look destabilized, she felt faint. She was disoriented to realize it saddened her that that's how he thought of her, as a sister. Then she smiled at her unintentional pun.

Seeing why her smile was sad, he said, "I hope this crisis of yours is an interesting one."

"I'll try to make it so."

"First we better eat."

"Did I ever tell you I think you order pasta primavera all the time in honor of the Botticelli?"

He grinned a surprisingly broad grin, then struggled to recompose his face. "Or tortellini in honor of someone's navel?" He was surprised how much Dolly had taken in. He was enjoying her plain goodness and humor. But now he noticed her roundly turned long legs, and she noticed he noticed.

For a while she looked into near space as young girls do when they're conjuring a response to a boy's sortie. She had not thought that Matthew would prompt her all the more to doubt her calling. Or had she?

From the first he'd spotted her flaw as a nun—she missed nothing, no one. He prepared to give Dolly his seriousness.

At dinner in one of those white-tile and polished-brass trattorias on Second Avenue they spoke of math.

"You taught math in high school, didn't you?" he asked.

"Oh yes, I love it, I delight in its certainties."

Matthew sipped his Corvo and was about to speak when Dolly wagged a forefinger at him, "Matthew, I do not, repeat do not, intend to talk about the Monod-Chardin thing."

"Actually it was fractals..."

"Matt!"

"No matter," he smiled, "like the Anglican heretics I'm always looking for the *via media*."

They basked in recognition of their liking for each other, their humorous minds rescuing them from darker musings.

As they left the restaurant, Matthew, feeling voluble after veal with figs and almonds, the specialty of his favorite Milanese chef, asked Dolly, "Did I ever tell you what I do for a living?"

"No, and I don't think you'd better now."

"I don't intend to," he said, mock-laconic.

As they walked she tucked her arm under his and tugged him off-stride in fun.

"I've always cast you as a casting director, Matt."

"Well, in a way I am."

"Then how would you cast me?"

"That's easy. As a Tuscan princess posing for a very old artist who has foolishly allowed himself to fall in love with her."

She looked at him, her lips parted in—what was it she felt?

"No, Dolly, I amend that: daringly, bravely, wonderfully, but not foolishly, I think."

They were quiet for a block or two. Her remark touched him.

"Oh, Matthew, what is there to do with such an answer? You can always be counted on to come in grinning from left field."

"It was a compliment."

"It was a dodge."

"Of course."

She shook her head in warm dismay. "Don't think I'm not going to ask you about this sister of yours. Is it an incestuous relationship?" She could scarcely believe she'd come to him sad.

"This from a nun?"

"Nuns can be curious."

"Yes, I think so myself."

They laughed and amiably teased each other on their way, and when they were home Matthew carried Dolly's suitcase into his own room and set it down under his heaven. Neither had spoken of where she'd stay and neither noticed what he'd done, or if Dolly had noticed she said nothing.

She walked first around his large foyer, then the living room.

"Richard Poussette-Dart, right?"

"Wrong! Mark Tobey, but I do like Poussette-Dart," he called from the bathroom.

It was only common decorum she not look, but Matt was speaking and where he was concerned Dolly's curiosity prevailed, so she peered around a corner to spot him before his toilet.

Any man who stands on one foot like a blue heron peeing into his toilet while pulling a sock off his other foot and engaging a nun in a conversation about Francis Cornish, the Robertson Davies art-restorer-hero of *What's Bred in the Bone*, is a trustworthy and good-natured man, she there and then decided.

"What is it you like about Francis Cornish, Matt?"

"Well, a woman he loved beat him up so badly he couldn't see straight, emotionally I mean, and he rebuilt his life with such decency and graciousness..." he flushed the toilet in lieu of completing the thought.

"Tobey?"

"Mm. Y'know he's a great painter of shore birds."

And while Dolly was musing that he must have caught her comparing him to a heron, he entered the living room with gorgonzola and Verdicchio and set them down on a glass and white wood coffee table. Dolly kept studying the walls, feeling a bit embarrassed to have peeked.

"How is Paolo?" she asked, seeing two of his paintings.

Matt was by the window sipping. Not at a loss for words, they were listening. To their own thoughts, perhaps to each other's, for we do, some of us, do that, but take care not to admit it because it is frightening.

"You know, a lot of men, most maybe, have only one woman in their lives. They go around having affairs, getting divorces, but there's just that one woman."

Dolly's fingers tightened around her glass. She was a hare frozen in a man's headlights.

"I know a guy who was fifty years old before he started noticing women who weren't blonde. You know why? Because his babysitter was blonde, a certain kind of blonde, cat-faced, so he only hankered for cat-faced, bowlegged blondes. I'm not sure that's living. It's like being half blind or half asleep."

Dolly listened to silence hum as Matthew paused. He didn't seem to be choosing his words—he didn't seem aware of them or of the silence between them.

"Take my mother, Maria. Can you imagine, can you even begin to imagine how in hell she chose a certifiable psycho for a husband? Didn't she know? Couldn't she tell? I sure as hell could. I mean, I think I was still in my crib when I started to feel endangered by Santo Pieto."

Silence.

"Did you hear me say it? Pieto? That's my name, my blood. So you know what I do? The minute a woman makes me feel a little crazy, just a little, I take a hike. Some people say a little crazy is love, so I guess that counts me out."

He noticed that Dolly was standing in the archway between the living room and his bedroom with its birth sky. She was studying his stars.

"You don't notice me taking a hike because fortunately for me most women just trifle with me. And since they haven't hooked me behind the navel the trifles may as well be truffles."

Dolly put her hand to her mouth to suppress a giggle, and for some reason Matthew found the gesture breathtakingly reassuring.

"I don't know what I'd do with a woman who made me feel crazy, kill her maybe. If you were me, would you take that chance? Hell no, you wouldn't! Santo's not out there where nobody ever heard of him again, he's in here." Matthew pounded his heart so hard Dolly could hear the thumps across the room.

She was thinking a lot of things to say, like maybe love and craziness are different, like nobody makes you feel anything, but she too feared Santo, and Santo was a man around whom it was best to keep your mouth shut. Or was it that Matthew needed to talk, or was it that he was doing her work for her, or deferring it, or was it their work?

She caught his look and she made circles of her thumbs and forefingers to peer up into his heaven. He smiled.

"It could be worse. A lot of men have mothers who hate them. Only God knows how messed up they are. I have a fool for a mother, but she's a good fool. I have a crazy for a father. And don't tell me about my grandfathers, I love them, but they don't make their living dry cleaning in Hoboken or driving bread trucks in Lodi."

Each word touched Dolly in a new place, like rain falling big and tentative at first, warm rain, pianissimo. It felt like being kissed. She drifted into the bedroom and began to unpack, no thought in her head, just the exquisiteness of listening like a doe in the wood.

"I'm reaching the age where you gotta have it together to get it up. I don't run like a steam plant anymore, and I dunno if I care."

Was that it, is that what he wanted to tell her, to tell someone? But it didn't feel like he was telling her anything. It felt like work. She couldn't reach out and be tender to him because he was doing the work, opening doors for her to walk through, making it possible for her to see what she'd come for. She must not stop him with anything like love.

Love?

"We're talking blood and I know where my blood came from, and I've seen what it wants to do: one half acts dumb and the other half wants to kill. This blood doesn't want to give anything to anyone, it wants to do things to people. I can't possibly be who I act like."

Dolly had stepped into the living room. The street lights passing through the window painted a geometric-abstract painting on the ceiling. She had never given a living soul the attention she now gave Matteo Pieto.

"Can I?" he said almost inaudibly.

He put his head on the back of his left hand, leaning against the window frame in a posture which in another man might have seemed tortured but in him seemed balletic and unspeakably sad. "I can't believe I'm saying these things. Dolly, how can you be anything but put off or maybe even scared by such talk?"

"Neither, Matthew, neither." She couldn't tell if he heard. She felt happy. Walking halfway across the room to him, she said, "I was thinking, well, in fact I've been thinking about my own sexuality, what it is, what to do with it, I don't even know if I want it. Can you really give it to the Lord? Give it away so it's taken and gone? Is that what God who loved a whore wants? I never asked myself these things until lately. Being a nun is so safe."

Now she saw his eyes widen. Dolly had Matthew's full attention.

"Does that scare you?"

"A little."

"That's nice, I'm glad I can do that."

He nodded respectfully.

"I see women throw themselves at you and you don't even seem to notice, you go on treating them like your best friend's mother."

"They toy with me and when they turn from the mirror they keep inside themselves, watching what they do, I'm gone, or they keep on toying with me as they walk out the door backwards."

Dolly spluttered her wine. "Oh Matthew, that's rare!"

She didn't understand what he meant about the mirror inside, she wasn't that sort of woman. She didn't know that some women use men like Matthew to witness their bad behavior. "You do have to give them a clue, you know."

"About what?"

"Where you're coming from. You know, your level of interest. I mean you have to help them. Do you help them, Matthew?"

He looked at her smiling for a long time, "When I think they have a message from the White Goddess."

"They all have messages from their mistress, Matthew. They just don't know it."

"You're wrong, Dolly. The goddess chooses her priestesses and messengers meticulously."

"So how do you tell if they do? I'm not going to ask you if you think I do, Matthew." And, having risked that, Dolly wobbled straight to a gaffe. "One thing I'm certain of is that I'll be one of the safest women in Manhattan tonight."

He felt dizzy, but he always had the pluck for courtesy. "What have I done to deserve such a compliment? Uh, it is a compliment, isn't it?"

She was nearly heartbroken to have afflicted this grand prince with anything so ugly and dumb, but she didn't know what to do except to go on teasing him.

"You know what I mean."

He didn't. He was miserable. But if he must feel this, better to feel it at the hand of such a guileless woman.

In the silence she heard her chance to bring their conversation to a point she was unaware she'd decided on.

"What is it that torments you so, that you can't just look up at the gods and say, Thanks?"

He looked up at Dolly Fitzsimmons, her flame-strewn hair, her pleasant hips and violet eyes made for the word comely. She blushed and like a novice poker player pressed her luck home to his.

"What is it, Matteo, that won't let you accept your luck?"

He looked at this unexpected guest, who'd unpacked under his heaven, and wondered if he had. That now he was working the crowbar in the crack he had no doubt. He looked about furtively; perhaps Titian's grandee was spying.

Dolly stayed on. A day or two became a week. A week, two weeks. By the third day she'd abandoned her habit for street clothing. On the fourth day they dined with Gran John, who decided within an hour that this was one Irish girl he could Italianize.

But when they were leaving, Maria took her son aside. She drew him under the staircase to her Lady altar, put his face in her hands and looked into his eyes gravely.

"Don't play God, Matteo. Let your grandfathers do that. She's married."

He shook his head, still in her hands, in incomprehension.

"To Christ. Let God decide, Matteo. That's very hard to do in our family. I know, believe me. I'm a nun too, aren't I?"

"It's not about Dolly, Mama."

"That's what you say, Matteo. But when you make a decision it's about everything that's going on in you when you make it."

"*Si*, Mama, that's right, but...."

"You want me to say it's about Billy? Okay, it's about Billy. Sure, it can be about Billy. Does that give you the right to disrespect the girl?"

"I would never disrespect her, I...."

"Think! You just happen to bring a nun to dinner in our house when Billy asks you a terrible thing and your grandfather says a terrible thing? *Spaventoso*, Matteo! You know it. I know it. You're my son. Don't act like a *soldato* who thinks he knows what women are good for."

~17~

As he freed the espagnolette bolt of the glass doors his shoulders and jaw jerked with cold intimation, as he slid his left hand down the sandstone balustrade to the street he felt his youth shrinking like Maria into that house, refusing to follow him.

In the next twelve days in the ease and graciousness of his nature he began to define himself. The canvas is chiaroscuro: darkness, rote and history on the one hand, and on the other inward search, profligate with its light.

Matthew knew how to move money, a thing by no means as easy as it sounds. He knew how to arrest large sums in their circuits and make them fall off the board without a trail. This he had studied more diligently than the history of Western art, making him something of a Merlin of money and both a diplomatic problem and solution, since he moved money for Gus as well as John and therefore had information each man swore to forego and nonetheless coveted.

He now set about moving a little over a million dollars through a maze of conduits into a Swiss account. He did this in a kind of reverie, taking responsibility he had never taken before, skillfully sorting monies he could call his own, examining his life's assumptions as if they were contraband goods, coming finally to the amusing recognition that he was not agonizing: his most defining characteristic had not left Maria's altar with him. He had become, for now, like the men he admired, John and Gus and Billy, men who lived in a world where uncertainty like as not got you killed.

To see a thing so clearly... the phrase began to haunt him. He'd put down a phone after a call to Milan and was saying to himself, "To see a thing so clearly..." then after a while amending it to say, "To know just what to do, to see a thing so clearly and know just what to do... is pathology!" he said the morning of the seventh day while shaving. Shaving like John, a strip of toilet paper over his shoulder, straight razor in hand, he walked to the bow window of his living room, arched his back and closed his eyes.

"Psychopaths!"

Psychopaths harbor no doubts, convinced that agonizing is for those who cannot see truth. He did not have the psychopath's freedom of action.

He closed the razor on his fourth finger, admired the brightness of his blood on the hardwood floor, and walked back to the bathroom as if he had received stigmata at the communion rail, numbed, elevated, wholly contained in himself for the first time in his life, and frightened.

The Saraceno puppet dangled remorseless in his bedroom closet. That, he decided, was its nature, to be remorseless. It hung on its cross in a space between his two best summer suits, its moustaches curved like its sword, eyes impenetrable. Like all idolaters of art, Matthew fixated on certain objects, smiles, gazes, expressions, turns of limb, qualities of light.

He knew but could not have said that there are faces in this world so beautiful as to terrify and others that remind us of the essential chaos behind our frantic efforts to organize the world and steady our place in it. Returning from this or that errand, he opened his closet to consider the Saraceno, deed of his great grandfather's hand, and each time he folded the doors on it he felt more disturbed than before.

On the eleventh day since their dinner with Gran John and Maria an explosion awoke them, Dolly in his bed, he in his guest room.

Sitting upright in bed, he said distinctly, as if instructed, "The hand that moves the Saraceno is cursed."

He sent for what he might have been dreaming. Nothing.

He went to the window. Nothing.

Dolly opened the door of his room. He was sitting cross-legged at the threshold. She wished, she knew she wished it, that it was for love. Maybe it was, but she could never guess that it was for love of a man too.

He craned his neck to look up at the fiery engine on his ceiling behind her shoulder.

"What was that, Matthew?"

"A truck or something," he said, not wanting to know.

She touched his shoulder as she passed. Then she went to the kitchen and made coffee, and with cup and saucer in hand wandered into his library.

Hundreds of books had burst from their shelves. Splinters of shelving, shards of vases and statuettes were everywhere.

She returned to her room. He was still sitting looking up at Paolo's engine. She put her hand in his hair. "Come with me, Matthew."

He surveyed the wreckage studiously, sipped from her cup, then walked back to his bedroom and opened the closet to stare at the baleful Saraceno.

If he harbored any irresolution, any fear of the volatility of his actions in the last eleven days, his fissionable library allayed them. Incurious as to its cause, he felt a mineral calm order his blood.

~18~

Dervishes of dogwood bracts danced in Gramercy Park as Matthew unlocked the south gate. Owning a building on the park's west side gave him the key.

As always Billy appeared from nowhere, half-smiling. They said nothing.

"John Garfield died in that house, the gray one," Matthew said. Billy smiled but did not turn to look at his friend.

"Are you remorseless, Billy?"

"So Matt, you decided to try a five-hundred-dollar word on me?"

"Are you?"

"Whuddid he die of?"

"He died in the saddle."

They walked about ten yards before Matt glanced to his right at Billy. Even in profile he saw grief in that face of planes and shadows, grief or... they walked another few yards when it came to him: loss.

"You don't like the question?"

"I like it, I like it."

"But not enough to answer it?"

"I like it too much to answer it. Besides, you don't want an answer, do you?"

Matthew pulled a heavy, cream-colored envelope from his jacket. As he'd so often done, Billy put it in his own jacket wordlessly.

"Open it."

Billy sat down on the south side of the little Victorian park. Banc l'Afrique du Nord, Zurich. M. Poule St. Nazaire. The raised letterhead reminded Billy of an incident in Dannemora. When he first got there some doughy wazoo, seeing him jiving with blacks, came up to him, spit in his hand and rubbed it on Billy's cheek.

"It don' come off, so you must be white. If yooz white, act white, do things the white way, got it?"

"Get this, prick," Billy had said, kneeing the guy's balls and ramming his flat head into a wall.

Matthew always did things the white way.

"What's this?" he pointed to a string of numbers written in Matthew's hand.

"A mil. A little more."

Billy leaned back on the bench, stretched his long legs into the white pebble path, closed his eyes and sighed.

"My grandfather says you deserve every penny. He says thank you and God bless you."

"What do you say, Matt?"

His eyes stung like New Jersey, his throat tightened. He saw now finally what he and Billy shared, always had shared, that still lust for staring life in the eye, he, Billy and Yeats:

Cast a cold eye / On life, on death. / Horseman, pass by!

"I had a brother."

As he rose Billy slipped a fine gold chain and cross from his neck and put it in his friend's hand. "You have a brother."

Then he looked at the gate and Matthew opened it.

Matthew joined the dogwood dervishes as Billy slipped down Irving Place like a submarine leaving Groton, turned right on Eighteenth Street, glanced left at Union Square, thinking of a surf of women's elbows in S. Klein's, walked across the park—where the young Matthew and his prep-school pal Arnoldo Christina used to listen to the marvelous leftist rantings of Slovene emigres—shrugged off Saint Francis Xavier School, faintly sinister, and, bearing down Sixth

Avenue to Fifteenth Street and the armory, inhaled an affair of charcoaled steak and marijuana from a sally port, heard high keening as mudejar as Appalachian, imagined a woman of indeterminate age in her great-grandmother's workday clothes, long-boned fair men in a weed garden... and thought of Connie Larimer.

He walked south on Seventh Avenue to Eighth Street, turned east past the Village Barn where high school kids from Bergen and Westchester celebrated their graduations, past MacDougal Alley and down into Washington Square Park where the chess games of old men were not as embittered as those in Union Square. Standing for a moment in the northwest quarter of the park and collecting the study of a demimondaine with two white poodles on troublesomely long leashes, he lost his way. He thought of a rose with root rot, he thought of the big nautical charts of the Mediterranean he'd been collecting, he thought of Hettie and swallowed hard, and then he remembered what to do, what Hettie taught him to do: make all sensibilities, the poignancy of fragrance and sound on Fifteenth Street, the crumbling woman and her poodles, all that he knew and felt of Matthew's gesture, the dying rose tree, every memory that ever would surface, make them all over into *prima materia* pouring through his hands into the krater, cooperating with the organizing intelligence of the cosmos.

Then what? Then your hands are washed of them, Hettie had said.

He did not fully understand this, and did not aspire to because he found the image restful and whenever he conjured it whatever followed seemed acceptable. So he turned right to where he could hear the Hudson pat the Plimsoll lines of behemoth ships made by men in envy of whales. Something in the straining of the lines aroused in him the foreignness of yearning. He began walking toward Little Italy. Lights and banners were strung across streets always celebrating something or someone. He slid like a pike in the reeds through the crowds of amblers and sidewalk cafe patrons, more than once casting a dour elephant's eye at some girl disquieting her companion to study him.

A man of obsessions could have conducted an interrogation, but Billy had no interior dialogue. He could not talk himself up and he could not talk himself down. Far from having a you in his head to direct him, he barely had an I. He had asked Matthew Pieto for the impossible and gotten it. So if he knew exactly what to do, as he thought he did, why was he stumbling around? Hey, Lorenzo di Credi is just taking a walk in Little Italy, right? He smiled. But in his head, far from painting a picture, he was wiring a device, tracing the diagram, looking for whatever would make it work.

What was it?

He bought an espresso and cannoli at Vincenzo's. Vinnie's smart-ass nephew held up his palm ostentatiously refusing payment. "How's the boss?" Billy stuffed two dollars in the man's shirt pocket, stared at him and walked out.

It was two when he realized he was three blocks south of Mina's. Through the three green rings of the neon Ballantine sign he saw Connie's face in the mirror surrounding the cash register. She looked gutted, abandoned. She looked up into the mirror and saw him for an instant before he moved on. A half hour later he was back, this time peering between two dead letters of a sputtering Ruppert's beer sign. It had been a rotten night, punks from New Jersey undressing her in their heads, cops busting up a fight, some Wall Street fox stiffing her for twenty-four dollars, and now she was getting weirded by Billy of all people.

She thought he looked like a little boy when he finally came to the open door. She felt moved, pissed, handled. Tears in her head ran around frantically trying to get out. She looked at him with her jaw jutting and, inspired at the last moment, put the fingertips of her right hand together and shook them at him in front of her face in the timeless Sicilian gesture of abject frustration.

Lorenzo di Credi blinked. Then he laughed. He laughed so hard his self-portrait shook on its hook. It felt like appendicitis. He blanched. Connie laughed. She laughed so hard and was so tired she wet herself. Then she tried to cry and when she couldn't she settled for watching him come to her, as if nothing that had ever happened to her mattered.

She poured him a tall glass of Saratoga water and when she turned to give it to him she saw that he had set a small map on the bar with three circled crosses: Tangier, Taormina and Malta.

"I wet my pants."

No such ploy ever deflected him, and his grave look, as it did so often, called the lost and playful girl in her and she started her long forefinger by her right eye down until it touched Taormina.

"There!"

Her heart raced, she could not look at Billy for fear of whatever was happening, so he took her finger between two of his until she risked looking up and he said, "Wanna come?"

The origins of the story

There are Mafia stories and there are Mafia stories, some too gory, some too romantic, some authentic, some baloney. This story, *Saraceno*, is drawn from the lives of two people, the writer, Djelloul Marbrook, and his stepfather, Dominick J. Guccione. Dominick knew Charles Lucana (Lucky Luciano), the Gallos, and a number of other mafiosi. His view of the Mafia was poignant. He was loath to talk about it. When he did he said, "When we came over here we wanted to leave four things behind: a corrupt church, a corrupt government, poverty and the Mafia—hey, three outta four ain't bad." But Dominick was an amazing autodidact and so he didn't leave it at that.

"When we got here," he said, "the Irish were in control of city government and they banged us around a lot. We thought fellow Catholics would maybe treat us right. That was a laugh. I'm deaf in one ear because one night when I was selling newspapers on Fourteenth Street an Irish cop clapped me on the ear for nothing. 'Get on with ya, ya little wop,' he said. So we needed something to help us deal with the Irish, and that happened to be you know who."

It was difficult in the 1950s in which the story is set to understand Dominick's view. The Irish and Italians had been intermarrying at that point for decades. But when the writer brought his first wife to meet Dominick the old warrior said, "What a pretty girl you are." Then his face turned pale and he said, "You're not Irish, are you?"

He didn't live long enough to see Italians play a major role in films and literature. But he might have known it was coming. By 1959, the year of his death, there were many policemen, lawyers and judges who were Italian-American. Frank Sinatra was already famous, as were Valentino and Caruso before him. Still the ascent of Robert De Niro, Francis Ford Coppola, Dom Delillo and many others would have surprised and delighted him. He probably wouldn't have been pleased by the *Godfather* movies and *The Sopranos*, but they would have been all too familiar to him.

It was from his life's experience and that of his friends that the Mafia atmosphere of this small novel is drawn.

But Billy Salviati comes straight out of the writer's experience selling newspapers at the corner of Forty-Sixth Street and Eighth Avenue. There he met and befriended a tall, pale young man very like Billy Salviati, and many of the scenes in the novel are drawn from their friendship.

Billy Salviati's story, *Saraceno*, is an allegory for our times. The nickname Gran John gives Billy in the book carries the entire weight of the West's history with the Arabs, a history of fear, misunderstanding, awe, and sometimes hatred. Billy roams Manhattan as the Arabs have roamed their deserts. He's not accustomed to giving or getting quarter. He's valuable, but misunderstood. The fact that he's half Irish leaves him outside La Famiglia, which he serves. His father's blood is not enough to make him an insider. He bears the name of outsiders whom the Sicilians admire, fear and remember in their collective unconscious.

The word Saracen, for all its venerable political baggage, has a bright origin. Etymologically the Saracens are "people of the sunrise," from the Arab word *sharqi*, meaning eastern, which itself derives from the word *sharq*, sunrise. It came into English via the Greek *sarakenos*, the Latin *saracenus* and the Old French *saracin*. By the time it arrived in English it was practically a pejorative, except in Sicily, where fond memories of Saracen rule lingered.

The origin of the word Mafia is less certain. It could be from the Arab words *ma afir*, the name of the Arab tribe that ruled Palermo. Or it could come from the Arab word *maha*, meaning quarry or cave. The Saracens fleeing European invaders hid in caves. It could even come from the Arab word *mafie*, referring to the tuff caves in the Marsala region of Sicily. No one knows for sure. One linguist describes a mafioso as "a courageous, brave fellow who won't stand any nonsense from anyone." Another associates the word with "boldness, ambition and arrogance." In any case, it wasn't generally used until the late nineteenth century. Sicilians, when they refer to it at all, have been known to call the organization The Black Hand or The Sicilian Protective Society. When the Federal Bureau of Investigation announced that it had finally learned the name of the crime organization and it was La Cosa Nostra, it was laughable because the cognoscenti had been calling it "our thing" for a very long time, and they didn't regard it as the official name of anything.

While Sicilian mothers were known to warn their children that if they misbehaved the Saraceni would get them, and while Sicilian puppet shows traditionally portray combat between Christian and Saracen knights, there is no doubt that Sicily's connection with the Saracens is richer and more understanding than in other European regions. The Sicilians, knowing they have Norman, Greek and Arab blood in their veins, are proud of it. So when Gran John in the novel *Saraceno* refers to his Saraceno he's summoning an immense trove of Sicilian and European history, and he's distinguishing Billy Salviati from among his soldiery.

Connect with the author online:

Website: http://djelloulmarbrook.org
Facebook: https://www.facebook.com/djelloul.marbrook.5
Instagram: https://www.instagram.com/djelloul_marbrook

Other books by Djelloul Marbrook:

Poetry
- *Far from Algiers* (2008, Kent State University Press, winner of the 2007 Stan and Tom Wick Poetry Prize and the 2010 International Book Award in Poetry)
- *Brushstrokes and Glances* (2010, Deerbrook Editions, Maine)
- *Brash Ice* (2014, Leaky Boot Press, UK)
- *Riding Thermals to Winter Grounds* (2017, Leaky Boot Press)
- *Air Tea with Dolores* (2017, Leaky Boot Press)
- *Nothing True Has a Name* (2018, Leaky Boot Press)
- *Even Now the Embers* (2018, Leaky Boot Press)
- *Other Risks Include* (2018, Leaky Boot Press)
- *The Seas Are Dolphins' Tears* (2018, Leaky Boot Press)
- *Singing in the O of Not* (2019, Leaky Boot Press)
- *The Loneliness of Shape* (2019, Leaky Boot Press)
- *Lying Like Presidents* (2020, Leaky Boot Press)
- *Dadaist and Dada That* (2021, Leaky Boot Press)
- *Once the Humans Were Gone* (2021, Leaky Boot Press)

Poetry and Fiction
- *Suffer the Children: Sailing Her Navel: Poems* and *Ludilon: A Short Novel* (2019, Leaky Boot Press)

Fiction
- *Alice Miller's Room* (1999, OnlineOriginals.com, UK; reprinted as title story in *Making Room: Baltimore Stories,* 2017, Leaky Boot Press)
- *Artemisia's Wolf* (2011, Prakash Books, India; reprinted as title story in *A Warding Circle: New York Stories,* 2017, Leaky Boot Press)
- *Guest Boy* (2012, Mira Publishing House, UK)
- *Mean Bastards Making Nice* (2014, Leaky Boot Press)
- *A Warding Circle: New York Stories* (2017, Leaky Boot Press)
- *Making Room: Baltimore Stories* (2017, Leaky Boot Press)
- *Light Piercing Water* trilogy (2018, Leaky Boot Press)
  I Guest Boy
  II Crowds of One
  III The Gold Factory